DEAD LION
by John & Emery Bonett

"Delighted me by its novelty, its ingenuity, its good-natured satire, and the general charm of its writing....Excellent entertainment with excitement thrown in." —*Bookman*

"A most civilized piece of escapism. It is urbane, amusing and readable...." —*The Sunday Times* (London)

Also available in Perennial Library
by John & Emery Bonett

A BANNER FOR PEGASUS

DEAD LION

by John and Emery Bonett

🌷 **PERENNIAL LIBRARY**
Harper & Row, Publishers
New York, Cambridge, Philadelphia, San Francisco
London, Mexico City, São Paulo, Sydney

DEAD LION

CHAPTER ONE

It was hard, in a way, on Cyprian Druse, that his death wasn't even dignified. To be found with his head stuck out of the window and the sash smashed down on his neck and the sash cords broken was unbecoming. He should have bled to death in the Roman fashion in a warmed and perfumed porphyry bath, or been stabbed by a jealous mistress, or simply crumbled away into horrible, overindulged old age. Even knowing so little of him as I then knew, I felt his last wish would have been that the commonplace manner of his death should be kept out of the papers. It was some time before I realised that the manner of his death wasn't commonplace at all, and was, so far as I could judge, as nearly what he would have chosen as any death could be.

My friends in America had told me how privileged I was to be going to England as the guest of my uncle Cyprian, "the Viking," whom I had never met. He was a celebrity, a member of the "National Quiz" radio team, one of the most brilliant living critics and men of letters, quite the most gifted talker. Americans still remembered his sparkling series of lectures before the war and how he had been fêted. One or two remembered how he had ridiculed American hospitality after his return and why he was never likely to be asked again; but they all agreed he was a lion of the first magnitude. And they all agreed that his appearance was as formidable as his reputation.

For my uncle, they told me, looked like a lion; more like a distinguished man of letters than even Tennyson or Bernard Shaw, and they, after all, had bolstered up the illusion with beards. But Cyprian Druse, clean-shaven and nearly fifty, was invariably mobbed at film premières by small boys who were certain that so much arrogance and poise must flower into an autograph that would dazzle their colleagues. He had the height, breadth, thrusting jawline and flaxen hair of a Viking, the scornful nostrils of a sculptured horse and the smile of a dissolute saint. My friends considered it amazing that such a man should bother to write at all. His ability to write so well seemed almost unnecessarily lavish on the part of his gods. The fact that he was a dead lion when I met him, however, tended in my eyes to level things a little.

Three people were at his flat door when I arrived from my taxi with a suitcase in either hand: the hall porter, the manager of Pendervil Mansions and Myrtle Best, the widow from the flat below, holding the glove which had been drying on her window sill when the drop of blood fell on it. That had started it. It ended when they opened the flat door with the master key and we found my uncle's body caught in the window with his chest and shoulders on the ledge and the sash smashed down on his neck.

There wasn't a lot of blood; just a greasy-looking trickle that had wormed its way across the narrow sill far enough to make one drip on the newly washed glove on the sill below. Mrs. Best was frightened but a little gratified, too, by her dramatic part in the matter. The manager was shocked but businesslike, summoning the doctor and the police on my uncle's telephone. The porter and I wrenched up the window between us. It had a huge, heavy plate-glass pane and wouldn't stay up without support, so the porter held it up while I brought my uncle in by the shoulders, and then helped me drag him over to the sofa. As I turned the body a bit of torn paper fluttered free from between the shoulder and the sill and settled somewhere behind the sofa.

My uncle's neck was broken, you could tell that. You could

see how it had been done, too. The porter explained that the sash cords had snapped a day or so back, and that while they were waiting for repairs he had supplied a wooden rod to prop the window open when required, as the weather was close. The rod was lying on the floor below the window. Cyprian must have propped the window open and, while looking out, have caught it with his shoulder and displaced it. The weight of the glass in the sash had done the rest.

The doctor came and pronounced him dead from the severance of the spinal cord; death having occurred about two hours previously, at approximately four o'clock. A police inspector arrived and examined the window and the dead man minutely, then the room and the desk. He questioned us all and expressed grave displeasure with me and the porter for disturbing the body. Having checked the arrival times of my boat and train, he asked what service my uncle had employed and was told that a daily manservant, Brady, came in to prepare breakfast and clean the flat, went home in the afternoons and returned about six-thirty to prepare an evening meal. The porter did not recall any lift passenger asking for my uncle's flat, nor had Mrs. Best noticed the door buzzer or any other sound to suggest that a guest had been admitted during the afternoon. The manager interrupted to point out that the flats were in all cases soundproof. Mrs. Best said so she had been informed, but on the other hand she *could* tell us that Cyprian had played the whole of Ravel's *Daphnis and Chloë* suite on the gramophone that morning.

A slight tension developed between them which was broken by the arrival of the manservant. The inspector explained what had happened. Brady was a catfooted young man with thickly fleshed eyelids and close-cut hair. His face twitched a little when he saw his master on the couch, but I could not tell with what emotion. He replied to the inspector's questions that he had left the flat at half-past two; that to the best of his knowledge his master had expected no guest except myself and had intended to remain at home until we left in the evening to dine with Professor Mandrake. He said that the window

11

was extremely dangerous and should have been seen to when he had mentioned it to the porter. The porter likewise passed the responsibility on to the firm of builders which, at protracted intervals, attended to the repairs to the building.

The inspector expressed himself satisfied that the death was accidental and that my uncle had been alone. The doctor made out his certificate and cracked some grim medical joke. The inspector handed back the glove to Mrs. Best, who somewhat reluctantly departed. He told me the coroner's officer would be along later that evening or early next day, to take depositions. It was only when they had gone that I realised that the body was to remain in the flat. Brady and I carried it into my uncle's bedroom and Brady showed me my own room and offered to unpack for me. I told him not to trouble. He then asked if he should prepare me a meal, but I said I would dine out and that he needn't stay. He gave me Cyprian's latchkey and asked if I would like him to come in the morning and I said yes, and let him go. I had no intention of being there in the morning nor any particular wish to be alone with the thing in the bedroom, but I was irked by his attentions and wanted to think.

I returned to the study and there on the sofa where it had been concealed by the body I saw something small and shining. I turned it over. It was a woman's clip-on crystal earring, carved in the shape of a wing. It must have been there when we laid down the body.

I dropped it suddenly, refusing to think. It might have been there for days, for all I knew, and it was nothing to do with me.

I had come to London to get Cyprian's name on a contract. Kirk, Appleyard and Cumfrey, the American literary agency to which I had been something like office boy before the war, had been slightly at a loss when I turned up after demobilisation, fit, fledged, half again the weight and three inches taller than when I left. But when Appleyard decided that a goodwill visit to England would be good for our contacts, he remembered that I was related to Cyprian and, by what means I was never certain, got the invitation out of him.

"Stay with him a fortnight," he told me. "Get his signature on our contract, and meet as many people as you can. We'll book a room for you at the Park Lane for the rest of the month you're in England. Your uncle may not be everyone's dish, but a couple of weeks under his auspices will give you all the contacts we want you to make and that we can't make for you. We'll see to the rest."

Cyprian was a literary exquisite. He wrote fewer words for more money than any man living. He could scorch up a reputation with a few sentences and he could make one, too, if he chose. He chose seldom. A satirist and a parodist, he himself was safe from satire and parody since he never produced any creative work but only destroyed. Like a blight, like a vampire, he fattened his reputation on the blood of his victims.

That was the man I had come to England to see. I had not expected to be met and I had not been. I knew enough about my uncle not to suppose he would behave like anyone else's uncle, but I had at least supposed he'd be alive. Now I was alone in a strange land with a strange body in a strange flat and I didn't mean to be there any longer. And I didn't have to be. My bags were still packed. I could take one in each hand, leave the key on the desk and never set foot on that exquisite carpet again. I felt in my pocket for the key Brady had given me, but my handkerchief got in the way, so I pulled it out. The key, which was caught in the folds, jumped out and skipped under an oak bookcase behind the sofa. I went on my hands and knees and felt for it, and as I did so I encountered something else, a scrap of paper, the torn scrap that had detached itself from between my uncle's shoulder and the sill as we turned him over.

It was a fragment of newsprint: part of three short paragraphs, headed in heavier type with "THIS" and another word beginning "EN——" There it was torn. On the other side was a bit of an article on lunacy. There were some papers on the desk and I looked to see which it had come from. Most of the periodicals had paper or lettering that differed from the piece in my hand till I came across a weekly without pictures, of exactly similar appearance. It was called the *New Statesman and Nation*. I flicked it open to find where the fragment had been torn from and my eye lit on the words "THIS ENG-LAND" in heavier type than the rest of the page, with a half column of short paragraphs below. That was where the "THIS EN——" of my scrap came from—but not from this copy. The copy on the desk was intact.

Perhaps the scrap was from the previous week's issue, I thought, but when I fitted it over the whole copy, the torn paragraph tallied. It had come from another copy of the same issue. There had been another copy of the paper in the room when my uncle died, and it was not in the room when we found him.

I wondered for a moment if the wind could have carried it out of the window, but it had been an exceptionally calm day and there was no wind at present. Besides, the bit of paper had been on the inside, crushed under his shoulder. If the whole journal had been caught under his shoulder and then torn by its own weight, it would have dropped to the floor inside the room.

The front page of the whole copy was dated the following day, Saturday. It could not have been on sale earlier than that morning. Of course he might for some reason have had two copies and thrown one away, but the wastepaper basket was empty and in the spotless kitchen I could find no rubbish of any kind. No, I felt sure of it, someone else had brought a copy of the paper to the flat that day; it had been on the window ledge when the accident happened, and someone had tugged it from under his shoulder and taken it away after his death. Only, however you looked at it, the death was accidental. No one could have planned the broken sash cord and the stick. And if anyone had been present, the natural thing to do would be to tell someone instead of walking out in silence—unless, of course, you had good reason for not wishing it to be known you had been there.

I began to be very curious about my uncle. I knew now that he was well over average height, with clear-cut features, beautiful hands and a cruel mouth. I knew that his mass of blond hair was very slightly touched up at the roots, and I should always think of his face as of a faintly greenish pallor, though that was neither here nor there. I remembered, too, something I had heard my mother, who had been his sister, telling someone long ago in a whisper—something that seemed all the more ludicrous in the light of his superb physique— that Cyprian had been born with a tail; just that embryonic stump like a budding horn that one in a million human beings can still discomfortingly be born with. He was single, nearing fifty, wore monogrammed silk shirts and lived well. How many people had loved him? I wondered. Would anyone cry for him; pray for him? And how many people, I was wondering too, had hated him enough to be glad of his death? I remembered another thing my mother had told from her childhood, how Cyprian had cut off the feet of a frog to see if it would still swim and had forced her to stay and count its strokes till it died—in the interests, as he assured her, of science. Yes, quite a number must have hated him.

Was there one who had hated him so much that when Cyprian had chanced to lean out of his window he had snatched the stick on an impulse and let the sash crash down on his neck; someone who had brought a copy of the *New Statesman* with him when he came and taken it away when he left?

My pulse quickened. It could even have been premeditated. If the visitor knew of the broken cords, he had only to persuade Cyprian to look at something in the street below. But why? I knew so little about my uncle although the room was full of him. His gaze met mine from half a dozen places: portraits, sketches, caricatures, a greenish bronze and an uncanny, gilded mask; all with the same fixed, hypnotic gaze which followed you everywhere. It was a cheap trick, of course, to impose his personality, but nonetheless he must have imposed it on the various artists of the portraits, none of whom

15

was a cheap artist. Charlatan, poseur, whatever you liked to call him, at least my uncle was in the top flight.

I shifted my eyes uneasily, for I was beginning to feel that he did not intend me to go, and that perhaps, through the wall of the bedroom, he was watching me just as intently. I reached for the grips of my suitcases and then jumped as the telephone rang. Half of me said, "Get out while the going's good or soon you may know too much to get out at all," but my hand let go of my suitcase and stretched out for the telephone.

"Hullo, Cyprian?" The voice was female, young, defiantly offhand.

I don't know why I had to prevaricate, but I said, "I'm afraid my uncle isn't available. I'm so sorry. Can I be of any use?"

"Oh—I didn't know Cyprian had a nephew. Are you—staying with him? Do you mean he's out?"

"Afraid so," I replied, still determined to give nothing away. "But isn't there something I can do?"

"Well"—the voice was cautious—"it's nothing really. Just something I—lent Cyprian that I rather wanted back. A gramophone record actually. I suppose *you* could let me have it, couldn't you?"

"Of course," I agreed. "Come on over and pick it out. I'll be here."

"Won't Cyprian be back? Oh, I mean—well, actually I'd rather not see him. It's—oh, just one of those things."

She didn't sound casual. She sounded wretchedly nervous. I tried to make up for it by the casualness of my reply. "Of course, of course," I said. "These things do happen. Come over any time before midnight and I promise Cyprian won't come barging in." And then, "Oh, did I have your name?"

"It doesn't matter," the girl said quickly. "I'll tell you when I see you, if you wouldn't mind. Oh, and don't bother to look out the record. I'll know it when I come. I'll have to be a bit late," she added. "I'm doing a show. Is that all right?"

"All right," I answered.

"You're sure Cyprian won't come back?"

"Sure," I said and she rang off.

My other hand still held the handle of the case. I put it down slowly, wondering why any gramophone record could be so important and why she was so afraid of Cyprian though clearly not of me, since she was willing to risk getting shut up alone, late at night, with whatever sort of wolf I might turn out to be. I had no idea what sort of relations my uncle had maintained with women. Now, driven by an irresistible curiosity to know something of his private life, I opened the drawer of his desk, but it was as neatly ordered as everything else in the flat. Note paper, clips, foolscap, carbons; no letters, not even any manuscripts, nothing personal of the man except his fanatical neatness. A tall wooden filing cabinet looked more promising. It had a roll front which was locked at the top. A little reluctantly I went into my uncle's room and came back with the bunch of his keys that Brady had put on the dressing chest when he gave me the latchkey. I found a small key which was clearly the right size but it wouldn't go in the lock. I tried some of the others but they were much too large. I tried the small one again and got it in a little way but it wouldn't turn. I took it out and, unbending a wire paper clip from the desk, inserted the end of the wire and twiddled it. In a moment I had coaxed out a twisted scrap of silverish wire, thinner than the paper-clip wire and wavy. I held it on the palm of my hand. It was almost certainly a bit broken off a fine hairpin. An odd little chill ran down my spine. Someone else had wanted to see the inside of that cabinet—someone who hadn't the key.

Now the key fitted easily and I dropped the roll front and exposed the labelled filing trays inside. But there weren't any letters or papers of any kind; just tray upon tray of gramophone records in thick paper folders. It was my uncle's unique and rather famous collection, mostly classical music, the labels lettered in the same meticulous, rather precious script in which my invitation from Cyprian had been written; the last little metal frame held a card which read, "These I have loved."

I drew out the tray and lifted out the records. There were

only six of them, and they bore no stamp or copyright sign of any of the great record-issuing firms but only a white disc of paper in the middle with "Polyphone-Vox Recording—Make your own records," and an Oxford Street address printed on it with a series of figures and dates in Cyprian's handwriting.

No need to search for the gramophone. It had towered over the room from the moment I entered, a monstrous thing with a hideous, handmade horn, the only ugly thing in the otherwise exquisite room, and, like most monstrous things, no doubt expensive. My hand was shaking as I put the first disc on the turntable, adjusted the fibre needle and placed it in the groove. I kept turning my head over my shoulder towards the bedroom, as though any moment I expected Cyprian to emerge and take exception to the unpardonable liberties I was taking with his property.

The record was nicked a little. It had been often played. It rasped on for a little too long before the woman's voice started, hurried, afraid, urgent. At times the voice grew too shrill for the recording and became only a squeak. The gist of it was clear enough and painful enough.

"You'll listen to me now," it said. "You'll listen now. It was the only way I had left. You sent back my letters; hung up on my telephone calls. Your servant always told me you were out. . . . I've got to see you. I've got to see you once. I won't plead or argue. I won't waste your time. I won't even cry—I've done enough of that, and you've told me it doesn't become me." Here the voice cracked a little and the speaker took a gasp of air. "You wanted me badly enough when I had no time for you at all. Now that you've spoiled me for anyone else, for anything else in the world that is decent and good and normal, now that I have no existence of my own except as some craven part of you—you can't throw me away. You can't. You've got to do something. I didn't even like you of my own accord, but little by little, with devilish ingenuity, you've destroyed me . . . so that the person who looks at me out of the mirror when I wake in the mornings is a person I cannot bear to live with—and I *do not intend to*. Do you understand? I

18

shall wait three days for you to answer, and after that it will be too late."

As I replaced it in the envelope I noticed a note in Cyprian's handwriting. "She didn't die, though," it said.

The next record was of another woman's voice, clearly not in such a state of tension; in fact it was even a little affected. After a few words I recognised it as the voice of the widow from the flat below, Myrtle Best.

"So you've asked me to make you a record," it said, "to write you a letter on a disc so that you can play it to yourself when you're alone, and think of me. . . . It's rather a sweet idea. I wonder why no one has asked me to do it before . . . But of course I don't. If you were not unique in everything you would not be you, the Viking, the one person in the world who understands me and sees me as I am. And because of this you know that when I am with you I am tongue-tied and inarticulate, but that alone with the disc and the thought of you, my heart can speak for itself—and for you, too. For of all those who come to you for succour and understanding, how many are there who in the least understand *you*? Not many, Cyprian. Oh yes, they envy your physical beauty and dread you for the philosopher and the cynic you are, the iconoclast and the shower-up of shams; oh yes, they have seen you giving and giving of yourself and of your genius all the time, squandering your fire, burning your candle at both ends—but how many have seen the sick small boy, grown tired of his toys, creeping home with the dawn, longing for rest and understanding and love?

"Well, now you will know there is one, and you will know that although your ecstasies and inspirations can be shared with none, at least there is someone who understands your darker hours of loneliness and longing."

Lightly scribbled across the label in pencil were three words, "The Sacred Cow," and it seemed to me that for once my uncle and I had been in accord and her pretentious silliness had not gone down any better with him than with me. I replaced the record in the envelope.

"My dear Cyprian . . ." The next voice was much younger; younger and also familiar. It was the girl I had just spoken to on the telephone. But it was even younger than that. A good deal had happened to this vulnerable creature between making that record and speaking to me this evening. "You have asked me to do something in particular," the voice went on, "and you have asked me to give you my answer in this way. You say that I owe it to myself and to my development in my career. You say that I am an artist and that an artist cannot afford to neglect any experience; that I must know myself and my own capacity to feel, to enjoy, to suffer, before I dare to set myself up in front of the world as Juliet or Ophelia, or simply as a guest of the Borgias. Perhaps I should tell you that your arguments have convinced me; but if I needed arguments to bolster up my intention to do what I want to do, I should be refusing to accept my share of the responsibility of what can only be mutual if it happens at all. You have taught me so many things about life, about beauty, about pain and about myself, that I want to learn this further thing as well and I want to learn it from you.

"Is this the answer you expected from me, I wonder? Has a little of the sadness gone from your eyes now that you have heard it? If not, perhaps I shall be able to smooth it away when I come. Good night, my dear."

Despite the sophisticated façade of what was evidently a very young dramatic academy student, the voice faltered and grew breathless in places. You could almost feel the terrified little heart beating out of the record, for all its high-flown phrases. I smiled a little savagely as I took it from the turntable. No wonder she wanted her record back. Poor child. Poor little silly; falling for that one about experience and acting. I had drawn a blank with that one at my first grown-up party, and a good thing too.

I found that from a passive dislike I was actively hating my uncle; feeling that if he *had* been permitted a natural death it would have been a bitter miscarriage of justice, but growing more convinced every minute that justice had not miscarried.

Someone, I was sure now, had killed him and then tried to pick the lock of the cabinet and remove the one thing that connected her with the crime, or with Cyprian at all. Not that in themselves any of the voices had so far suggested a capacity for murder, but they certainly suggested a motive—and I hadn't heard them all.

The next had "Lisle Street" pencilled on the label. As I placed it on the gramophone, the telephone rang. It was the management of the flats, wishing to know if I had made arrangements for the night and offering to place a service room at my disposal if I preferred it. Evidently they were scared that I might consider the window-sash business to be negligence on their part and might make difficulties or occasion more publicity than was desirable. I assured them that I was content and declined their hospitality. It was not till I had hung up and was back at the hideous gramophone that I realized how I would have welcomed the suggestion a short while ago. Nothing was going to stampede me out of the flat now, until I had at least heard the rest of the six records; nor then, if I could help it, until I had met the women who had made them and had a chance to decide why Cyprian had died. Impatiently I lowered the needle to the disc.

A very few revolutions proved this one to have been made by a West End drab. An artificial refinement was laid heavily over the original coarse accent, and the voice, devoid of humour or personality, reiterated that she didn't do "this sort of thing" really, in fact she thought it rather *"ostentious and conspicious,"* but that as Cyprian had treated her like a gentleman she was obliging him by making the record at his request. It was the dullest of them all, giving no indication of the woman's character, and only adding to the portrait I was building up of Cyprian the fact that at some levels he maintained the schoolboy's sniggering approach to sex, finding something smart or shocking in the mere fact of his acquaintance with a woman of professionally easy virtue.

Clipped to the fifth disc was a newspaper cutting. I detached it and put on the record. It soon became clear that it had been made by a poetess and sent to Cyprian along with a volume of her verse, as a sort of dedication. It was a nervous, rather high-pitched voice, a little girlish in a cultivated way but with no youth in it. "Of all the poems I have sent you," it ended, "the best is the last; the one I have called *Immaculate Despoiler*. You will know for whom that one was written and perhaps it will help you to understand."

The clipping proved to be an article signed by my uncle, from a literary review, criticising a volume of verses by a woman poet, Cynthia Spalding. I would not have given much for her peace of mind when she had read it. It was hard to believe that any man could take the infinite pains my uncle must have taken, to build up something so that he could have the perverse pleasure of destroying it. More than ever I felt that whoever had taken a hand in his death had rid the world of a disease.

The last record was a revelation. Of them all, it had the only voice which sounded mistress of the situation, totally in command of itself, even laughing a little at itself and at Cyprian. It was a slow, smoky voice that sounded as though it might have been combed back from the dead, but it was a voice young in years, a deep, rich voice whose very whisper might have caressed a dying man to vigour or turned a living man to a swine or a god.

"So you want me to make you a record too," it began, "to add to your collection. Just for your ear alone, you told me, but you forget how much I know. You forget that I know you play them over to a few selected spirits of your own kind on evenings when other sensations pall. That first poor girl gave you the idea, didn't she? Oh yes, that gave you a kick, Cyprian, didn't it? She promised to die for love of you. No one else quite came up to that for sheer sensation, did they? But even she let you down and lived, though you raised no finger to help her and were willing to let her die. So you asked the others, one by one, to make you records, and they did; but the others just bolstered up your ego a little and did no more. I'll try and do more for you than that, Cyprian.

"But I think you won't play my record over to your friends. I think you won't. You see, I understand you. I wasn't so easily impressed as the others, so to shock me you told me what started you off, hurting and destroying. There's something ludicrous about you. So that you were laughed at by your first love. So that your soul twisted inside you and you shut yourself away for many years, hating, and formulating plans of revenge against all women and all normal, healthy men. You wanted to torment and destroy, and you succeeded very often, for everything you touch is poisoned, and the people you have at any time loved are left with a little poison somewhere in their systems, a little blight that may not appear till the flowering. And now you want to destroy me.

"You're flying a little high this time. My brain is clear and I can see through you and know you. And because I can see past your magnificent appearance into your twisted, tormented soul, I can pity you. But more than that, I am afraid of you; afraid of what you can do to me and of what you can make me do, for I think you have some kinship with the devil. But you're ruthless and in some measure honest, and so, perhaps, am I; and you haven't a particle of sentiment in you nor, I'm sure, have I. And though I fear you as I fear the devil, I do not stay away.

"You won't play this record with the others, will you, Cyprian? I think you won't. It tells too much. You could break it very easily, but you won't do that either, since here is the kick that you looked for in vain in the others—for though you have never touched me and I intend that you never shall, and though you are chaos and old night and the bottomless pits of hell—it seems that I am in love with you, Cyprian, God help me; and I shall have no peace from you till you or I are dead."

Almost at once, before the record had run half a dozen turns round the table, I was a lost man. This is it, I thought. This is the woman. This is the "green light under that sycamore tree," and Circe and Helen and my own especial doom. Come life, come death or hell-fire, I should have to find the owner of that voice. Find her and then discover some way of arresting her attention; for you didn't have to tell me it wasn't going to be easy for any little pip-squeak who hadn't got anywhere yet. We weren't halfway through the record before I knew I hadn't yet got anywhere, nor been anywhere, nor amassed any experience of life that might entitle me even to her casual interest.

And then it occurred to me that I had her record. And that might entitle me to *some* interest if it had been worth Cyprian's death to her. For just as surely as I knew she was for me, I was also sure that, out of all the voices I had heard, hers was the only one whose owner could have killed him.

None of the others had the force, the sureness of touch, the character, to carry out a crime and get away with it. So far had I strayed already from plain sanity that I found I was despising them for that; comparing them with her and finding them wanting. In their love, in their grief, in their gaiety or in their pain they were probably genuine enough; only their voices didn't send my heart knocking against my ribs as hers did, and I knew that if all the angels in heaven stood between us with their bright swords I had to find her.

"Stay out of this," my head was telling me. "You've got your future and your job to think about. All right, your uncle's death wasn't an accident, but even from the little you know about him it was overdue and good luck to whoever did it. He's dead and the law is satisfied. You don't have to prosecute. You don't have to hunt down the criminal either. You don't have to do anything. If that girl did it, she had her reasons in plenty, but she did it just the same. Leave her to her conscience and any luck that can come her way, but leave her alone. She's got blood on her hands."

Only it wasn't particularly her hands I was curious about, no, nor her body either, but the woman herself. I wanted to know her, to see her move about a room; to see her in repose when she thought no one was there. I wanted to know if Cyprian had died in time and if she was free of him, or whether he haunted her dead as much as he had alive. Oh yes, I wanted the feel of her in my arms, too, but most of all I wanted her there, just standing in the doorway, where the light of the lamp didn't quite reach her—and it seemed to me that I knew how I could get her there.

So while my brain retold me the folly of getting mixed up in the matter my hand reached for the telephone directory and presently I called up the *Daily Recorder* and asked for "Subs" and finally for Robert Dent. I hadn't seen Robert since we were in the desert together but I knew he was a sub-editor on the *Recorder*. I got him fairly easily. When the enthusiasm of our reunion had spent itself I said, "Did you know Cyprian Druse is dead?" And he said, "His obituary's been set up half an hour. Tell me something I don't know."

"Did you know he was my uncle?"

Robert hadn't known that. His warmth was sudden and ingratiating, when he realised that he'd been deloused side by side with the nephew of the day's most celebrated corpse. "Got any dope?" asked Robert.

"Only that he's left me nothing but a dreary collection of old gramophone records."

I felt Robert's interest quicken. "His records?" he said. "I wouldn't grouse. That collection is world-famous. He mentioned it on the air pretty frequently, too. Why don't you sell it?"

"Sure," I said. "I'll sell. They don't mean a thing to me. Anyone can have them who'll pay for them. Privately, though —I don't want to be bothered with dealers."

"There might be a paragraph in that, not more," said Robert, his interest flagging. "Where are you staying?"

This was the last point I had to make. "Oh, I'm roughing it in his flat for a day or two," I told him. "I'd just arrived on a visit when they found him."

"How did they find him?" asked Robert, his ears pricking up again. "How did he die?"

"Accident," I answered, and rang off.

And now it was done. For if there were something in that record cabinet that it was worth murdering Cyprian to destroy, it would be worth a visit to a lackadaisical nephew who didn't care enough about music even to play over the records, to try and get it back. She would come; so, for that matter, might the little actress and any number of other people, but *she* would come and I should see her. The possibility that she might shoot me could not, of course, be altogether ruled out, but I didn't imagine she was an habitual criminal. No, she had come to plead with Cyprian for the return of her record or for letters or because she couldn't resist the hideous fascination he had for her—he had happened to lean out of the window and her eye had fallen on the prop and she had thought, "How easy . . ." When she visited me, I needn't look out of any windows.

Only this time she would know what she was doing and she had to get that record before anyone else played it. Whatever I said, she wouldn't be quite certain that I hadn't played it; so this time she might have a little gun about her person. Just a little mother-of-pearl gun, I liked to think. I was as sentimental as a schoolgirl about the whole thing. Of course the gossip paragraph in the *Recorder* wouldn't come out until next morning, and even then she mightn't see it. If it failed, I could advertise the private sale of the collection of records in the *New Statesman*. My uncle's murderer certainly read that. But that meant delay and possible complications. My uncle's will would have been read by then and someone would have noticed that he hadn't left his records to me at all.

There was quite a bit of time before anything might happen, but on the other hand, if I went out now, it might just happen before I got back. Besides, she'd have missed her earring by now. A girl like that, who'd been beaten when she had only a hairpin, wouldn't be above coming back with a set of skeleton keys. I had every confidence in that girl.

I decided not to leave the flat and rang down to the restaurant for some food; then I switched on the radio just in time to hear an intimate voice saying, "That is the National Quiz Team and here are the questions. . . ."

"Mrs. Braddock of West Hartlepool writes," came the question master's smoothly groomed voice, " 'Man's love is of man's life a thing apart; 'tis woman's whole existence' is widely quoted. Does the National Quiz Team agree with this, and if so, why?"

There was a pause during which one sensed the listening world groaning for the bathos of the question and thinking how much better questions it could have sent in if it could only find the time.

"Mr. Druse?" said the question master.

"Love," came the mellow-golden voice which must be that of the man whom I knew to be dead on his bed a few feet away from me, a voice that despite its caressing softness rasped the nerves and lifted every hair on my head, "does not exist."

CHAPTER TWO

"Good lord!" I thought and ran headlong into the bedroom, but the figure lay stiffening there on the counterpane. I shut the door quickly and came back and found the *Radio Times* on the desk. Friday, yes, of course, "Recorded session of last Sunday's National Quiz Broadcast." Then a list of the team of which my uncle, as I knew, was a resident member. I sat down again with the paper open as I listened with a mixture of horror and pity to Cyprian Druse, unmindful of his end, throwing off fireworks and turning his plumage this way and that to catch the rays of his so soon setting sun.

Perhaps they didn't know he was dead, I realised; perhaps *I* ought to have let them know. The *Daily Recorder* had known when I rang, presumably through the police, so the B.B.C. must know, though it had been too late for the six o'clock news. Perhaps it hadn't got through to the other departments, or they'd decided to run the recording anyway and had made an initial announcement which, tuning in when I did, I hadn't heard. Mr. Druse was qualifying his statement. "The human race," he went on in the fanatically happy voice of one who is about to deprive a saddened world of its last toffee apple, "is inspired or tormented by a thousand different emotions, urges and reactions, all of which are lumped together by popular usage under the main heading of love. All of them are, admittedly, in a sense, expressions of love, but love of self only, in other words, greed or a desire to perpetuate. If I could find out of my whole life's experience one example of genuine, selfless love, how happy I should live, how happily, indeed, I should die. But romantic love, as it is imagined to exist between one human being and another, is a myth."

"I fancy that dissentient voices are about to be raised," said the question master. "We must accept for the present that Mr. Druse has never been in love, and hear what Major Pethwick has to say."

The major could be heard clearing his throat. "Can't say I agree with Druse," he said in a bluff, kindly, willing-to-be-corrected voice. "I'm only a plain man and you may laugh at me when I say I've had some very real experiences of love in the romantic sense and I can claim quite definitely that it does exist." He paused for the hearts of plain men and pretty women to warm to him all over the country, then went on, "After all, it's an old saying, It's love that makes the world go round, and if you just think about it, where would any of us be without it?"

"Major Pethwick is in favour," said the question master archly. "Professor Mandrake?"

I looked at the *Radio Times*. In the corner of the page there was a photograph of Mandrake the anthropologist, a man quite strikingly ugly who wore his skin like a baggy suit. Beside it was a photograph of a woman I liked at sight. Roughly in the forties, with hair and clothes arranged in no particular way, with no great pretensions to smartness or good features, she had an expression of such calm good-fellowship that it was difficult not to smile back at the photograph. The caption told me she was Mabel Grey, the Member of Parliament for Wrottesley, and a resident member of the National Quiz.

In a rumbling, badly co-ordinated voice, which seemed at times to come from different directions, Professor Mandrake was pointing out that so far no one had made any attempt to answer the question, which was the essential differences between a man's way of loving and a woman's. At this point Pethwick came in from a new angle to polish off the actual question—as distinct from the one he had answered—before anyone else had a chance. Major Pethwick bluffly asserted that there was no getting away from the facts, since nature had arranged for man to be the fighter, the pioneer, the thinker, and that naturally his interests were wide and took him outside the home; whereas for the woman, her mate was her adventure. The question master called on Mabel Grey. It was a warm, friendly voice which I seemed to have known all my life, though I'd certainly never heard it before this moment.

"I'm afraid there *may* be some truth, at present, in that quotation," admitted Mrs. Grey, "and inasmuch as there is, it's dreadful; it's got to stop and it will be stopped. For any one human being to be another's whole existence is unhealthy for the one who loves and intolerable for the one who is loved. It can only happen where women are not educated to take an intelligent part in the world about them, and it's up to every one of us to see that at least in the next generation there are no women in that degrading position."

"Mrs. Grey thinks it's true but it's a pity," threw in the question master, before yielding up the field again to Druse.

"If we must assume," my uncle's voice softly persuaded the world, "that the emotion referred to in the poem *is* in fact love, which I deny, and not a biological urge, which I submit; if we must accept this term for want of a better, we must agree that in love the sexes are totally different. The male wishes to possess, to perpetuate himself and then discard. The female requires above all things to give. For her this is vital. She wants to be convinced that she is necessary. If she is married to a man whose independence of her is unassailable, she will find some other man, woman or child, even a cat or dog, upon whom she can shower attentions to the limit of her powers—entirely without reference to the merit of the object of her devotion. In fact, it is the theme of my just completed volume, *Analysis of a Woman 'in Love,'* that if a woman cannot find an object for this overpowering passion to squander herself, she will invent one which doesn't exist and squander herself upon that. I might add that I put the words 'in Love,' in my title, between inverted commas, and that, despite our question master's earlier quip at my expense, the experience of falling therein is one which I have permitted myself on many occasions, though I do not dignify the emotion involved with the vexed word, love."

"Mrs. Grey," said the question master almost before Druse's voice was silent, and she danced in like a fencer, with all my money on her.

"Mr. Druse," she said, "must be his own judge as to the dignity of his own emotions, but I venture to speak for the dignity of the race in general." You could feel the tension of the electric storm that flashed around the table, but her voice was cool and assured and without malice. She was trying to give back to the world what he was trying to take away. "Love exists," she continued, "and it ennobles. Oh yes, I agree that it is better to love something imperfect than to love nothing at all, and I admit that we need to love something if we are to reach the heights to which only we can climb; but it is not a figment of the imagination nor is it all base, petty, nor to be explained away in a few cruel, polished phrases that stay in the mind and baffle the heart and cripple the aspirations. All through the ages men and women have worked in the dark for no reward or fame, for love of humanity, love of God, and plain human love of one another. Look at the air raids, look at the battlefields, look into our own lives. Explain it, belittle it, deride it—love exists and will triumph, and we can thank God for it."

The question master was getting a little embarrassed. "Well, Mrs. Braddock of West Hartlepool," he said, "I think you've had your money's worth. Major Pethwick and Mrs. Grey are for it. Druse is against it but admits he has had his moments. The next question comes from Ernest Robinson in the Outer Hebrides, who writes, 'I never can bring myself to eat butter when it is the strong yellow colour which most people prefer, but only take it when it is a pale creamy shade. Is it true that colour in food has any effect on our digestive systems?' "

I felt the tension of the unseen battleground relax to butter consistency. The telephone rang.

I lifted off the receiver and my ear was filled with a bellow that sank to a whisper. "Mandrake here," said the voice. "Where's Druse? I expected him to dinner."

"Good lord," I said. "Didn't anyone tell you? I suppose I should have. I'm terribly sorry."

"Sorry about what?" asked Mandrake. "Who are you?"

I told him what had happened.

"Oh," he said. "Yes, he was going to bring you too, if you arrived today. Sorry about Cyprian. Bit queer for you. Only just arrived in England, hadn't you? D'you know anyone? Are you on your own?"

"Just about," I admitted.

"Come over here for the rest of the evening," he suggested. "I'm afraid we've had dinner now, but there'll be something. Depressing for you on your own."

But I didn't want to leave the flat. I was determined not to leave the flat. Somebody wanted one of those records badly, and there was quite a chance that person was watching the flat and would be round in an instant, once I had been seen going out. On the other hand, I wanted to meet Mandrake very much, or indeed anyone who could tell me some more about my uncle. I told him so and without going into all my reasons asked if he felt inclined to reverse things and come over to me for a drink. He accepted my invitation, whether out of kindness or curiosity, I couldn't judge.

As I went to the pantry for glasses and some of my uncle's sherry I could hear Cyprian's voice discoursing on the pleasures of the table and I shuddered again very slightly. The food arrived from the restaurant and I carried the tray back into the study, leaving the lights switched on in the passage so that I might at all times be sure that the shapes and shadows of furniture and doorways with which I was not yet familiar *were* merely the shapes and shadows of furniture or doorways.

I ought to have switched the radio off if I had hoped to enjoy my meal, but I felt compelled to hear my uncle's last words on euthanasia and, later, on the desirability of war to offset the increased longevity of the race brought about by the improvement in medicine and hygiene.

Mandrake loomed in just as the broadcast was finishing, shabby, vast, amorphous, his feet seeming to be not quite in contact with the earth, and wearing in his buttonhole a huge yellow carnation that gave him the appearance of a cactus which had shyly burst into flower. While I poured the sherry he asked if I had been fond of Cyprian.

"I never saw him alive," I explained. "How did you get on with him?"

Mandrake was too far gone in his profession to be overmuch a diplomat. "Human beings are my raw material," he said. "To permit myself to form attachments for them would be as disastrous as for a vivisectionist to become a member of the R.S.P.C.A."

I said, "A definite dislike would not be so disastrous, and would be more natural in some circumstances—judging by what I have already learned of my uncle."

"More natural, yes," admitted Mandrake, sinking into a square-armed leather chair. "His was not an endearing personality, but it will make itself missed."

"Would you call his death a loss to the thinking world?" I asked. "Was his influence, if any, good or bad?"

"On the thinking world he had no influence whatever," said my visitor. "Cyprian Druse was a charlatan. But his influence on the man in the street was immense and dangerous."

"Did they take him as seriously as that?"

"Not consciously, no; but he had a way of telling them what they wanted to hear in a phrase they would remember, even though they forgot whose phrase it was. But besides that, Druse was eaten by a worm. He saw things crooked and he spoke for crooked people with such eloquence that they believed he and they were normal and the rest perverse. He had a poor stomach but he championed the pleasures of the table; he championed lust with such ardour that I have been tempted to suspect he was but a poor performer. He hated women. I think he was afraid of them."

"Do you think it possible," I asked him after a moment, "that he might have failed in some signal instance, made himself ridiculous, perhaps, at some moment of his most intense sincerity, and that ever since then he's been trying to take it out on the whole sex; shouting to keep his courage up; trying to convince himself, or at least everyone else, of his own superiority?"

Mandrake put his sherry glass on the arm of his chair and looked at me with close attention. "Yes," he agreed, "something like that; something very much like that indeed."

I said, "Did you know my uncle had a tail?"

He pondered the matter. "Not a very big one, surely?" he asked.

"Not very," I answered, "but a quite small tail might humiliate one in certain circumstances, especially if the other person concerned were unaware that human beings could be born with such a formation, and became embarrassed or shocked."

"An early love affair, you mean?" said Mandrake.

"Yes. Suppose Cyprian to be a person highly strung and intensely nervous and so conceited as to be almost entirely at the mercy of other people's opinion of himself—mightn't his humiliation crystallize into a hatred of womankind?"

"It might," agreed Mandrake. "It very easily might. Though your uncle didn't hate all women. There is a type with which one is forced to believe he had a very considerable success: sensation-loving women, careerists, pseudo-intellectuals who fancied an affair with him would get them a little publicity; oversexed, mentally retarded women who bolstered up his own belief in his virility. It was the other type he hated."

"What type?" I asked.

"Gentle, affectionate, contented women who wanted nothing from him and had nothing to give him. Dull women, he'd say; respectable women with no history, the sort you and I would choose for our wives and our mothers, happy women. Cyprian Druse hated happiness."

"He sounds the most unhappy man alive."

"Perhaps he was; perhaps that was why he loved to expose what people thought was happiness and show it up for something very much less. That was the basis of his perpetual duel with Mabel Grey."

"Mabel Grey of the National Quiz?"

"You know her?" His almost inhuman, pale eyes focused on me acutely.

"No. I heard her for the first time on the air tonight. I felt as though I knew her rather well."

"That is the thing about her; everybody feels as though they know her rather well. She's the woman in everyone's chimney corner; the sane, unflurried member of every family, who can be appealed to for fair play. People write to her about their loneliness and their in-laws and about Ronnie having an affair with That Woman."

"I know what you mean," I said. "I felt I could tell her anything."

"Most people do," said Mandrake, "not just feel they could, but actually sit down and write to her about it. She always answers, too, though it must take far more time than she can spare."

"Isn't that always the case?" I asked. "If you want an answer by return, write to someone whose every moment is filled with important work. I suppose besides her career she's got a hard-working and adoring husband, a nursery full of healthy, brawling children, and probably a younger brother she's seeing through college as well."

"No," Mandrake answered slowly, the smile fading from his face. "She hasn't any children. There was a niece she was very fond of whom she brought up, who ran away or turned

34

out badly, I don't know exactly; and the husband drinks. But no one would suspect any of that."

"No indeed," I answered. "I've never heard anyone who sounded more sure of themselves, more happy and fulfilled."

"Nor I," said Mandrake. "Especially during the last six months or so."

I refilled our glasses in silence, hoping he would go on, and in a moment he did.

"Mabel was always sane, balanced, free from malice, but before it seemed to come from a profound, inner loneliness, a sharpening of the perceptions through pain and a deep detachment; a sort of pity for humanity. But lately I've felt that she wanted to bless and to bestow on the world some of the happiness that was brimming inside her; as though she had stumbled on the concrete truth of everything she had hitherto been trying to believe in the dark."

"Do you mean religion," I asked a little doubtfully, "some sort of faith?"

Mandrake regarded me mournfully. "Religion could do that for some women," he admitted, "but she's grown prettier too, and she holds her head better. I think she must have fallen in love."

Something in the wistful, hangdog look of his not entirely anthropoid head suggested to me that Professor Mandrake deplored the possibility.

"It sounds like the best thing she could do," I said, "if her domestic life is so unsatisfactory. But is there anything to support the idea?"

"Not very much," said the professor, "but a little. I think I was the only one of our team that she ever talked to. No"— he smiled rather disarmingly, though not at me—"she wasn't interested in me. We both caught our trains from the same station, and sometimes, after we'd left Broadcasting House on recording day, she'd have a cup of coffee in the waiting room before her train came in. I got into the habit of joining her."

"Where does she live?"

"At Barrow Lock; that's on the river. My station was

Kelving, not more than three miles away but on a different line. I never went to the house."

"You just saw her in the station waiting room, and at the B.B.C."

"Yes. There's a rather famous pub at Barrow Lock, the Sitting Hen. Druse and his lot used to go there a good deal for week ends. They did a superb chicken-and-mushroom pie even in wartime. I walked over there sometimes on Sundays. Her husband was usually in the bar but I never saw Mabel there." He seemed lost in a reverie of wasted Sundays. I said, "And this other man?"

"One day she was writing on a pad when I found her in the waiting room. I sat down rather clumsily and knocked her papers on the floor. As I handed them back I read 'Colin, my dearest,' at the top of a page. She coloured up like a girl and covered the pad as I apologised. I felt I was butting in and moved away to the counter and stayed, drinking my coffee there. She didn't even notice that I didn't come back. She had everything in life that she wanted, there at the marble-topped table in the station buffet. I remembered then that recently as we had sat together, warming up and waiting to begin the broadcast, she had a letter in her hands, that she might glance at and smile, but which she seemed to know by heart, only liked to keep her hands on, as though it were a talisman. And sometimes when she'd ridden into a discussion on the side of the angels, and risked the awful stigma of being an idealist, or even a Christian, her eyes would widen and she'd give a gallant little smile and grip the letter. I realised now that this must be because Colin, her dearest, was somewhere listening and that the knowledge had given her courage." Mandrake looked at his hairy, spatulate-fingered hands rather sheepishly. "It is a part of my profession," he explained, "to know why human beings do as they do."

I agreed gratefully. He had told me a good deal about why human beings did as they did; one in particular. He had told me he was in love with Mabel Grey.

CHAPTER THREE

I said, "And Mrs. Grey, in particular, represented the type of woman towards which my uncle was antagonistic?"

"She was serene," he answered slowly, and his face, of which not one feature could be described as in any way pleasing, was lit by such warmth of affection that I had no difficulty at all in feeling fond of the man. "He couldn't scratch her serenity. She believes good is greater than evil and that human beings are capable of making themselves something more than animals scrambling greedily from the cradle to the grave. She believed there was something divine in us all, even in him, and she had the courage to say so. While he was talking, he could cut circles round her, and reduce every emotion in the world to greed or a desire to perpetuate; he could show her up for a sentimentalist, with no logical or biological basis for her convictions at all; only after the fireworks, somehow, the feeling persisted that though he was brilliant she was right."

"You thought she was right, yourself?"

"Thought? I? Oh no, I knew she was wrong. Knew it with all the weight of the knowledge I've amassed in my lifetime. But the one thing you learn, if you're capable of learning anything, is that you can't *know* anything. So in spite of all I knew, I suppose I *felt* she was right."

"But not with your brain. Felt it in your heart, perhaps?"

"The heart," he snapped suddenly, "is an elaborate arrangement of muscles and cells for pumping the blood through the body. Feeling is not its function."

I raised a caustic eyebrow to goad him, though I have never liked a man better than I was liking this one while he struggled

37

to coin a biological expression that would cover the soul without leaving himself uncovered.

"I suppose it is something to do with the spirit," he said. "Anyway, I prayed that she was right and the rest of us wrong. But I had to join my voice against her."

"Along with Druse?"

"Not entirely, no. At least I am impersonal; but Druse's whole intention was to discredit women. His great cry was, 'Women don't think, they only feel.' His scapegoat was feminine intuition. He proved over and over again that woman was inferior to man, but yet, at the end of a session, he never left us in any doubt that he was an inferior being to Mabel Grey. I think he would have given everything he had to discredit and humiliate her and prove her the tool of his trinity, sex, greed and the desire to perpetuate. But she seemed to love humanity and to include him in it, so she always had the laugh on him."

"That must have been singularly hard to forgive."

"To be loved impersonally, on the grounds that one is, after all, one of God's creatures," agreed Mandrake, "is most unsatisfactory. It happens to me a good deal," he added without rancour.

"Did my uncle boast to you about his women?"

"No. He could talk brilliantly on a number of subjects and he hated a slipping audience. When he started on women I went to sleep."

The door buzzer sounded.

"Are you expecting anyone?" asked Mandrake, and without thinking, I replied, "No." He went to the door. I looked at my watch and saw that it was after eleven, and I remembered the girl on the telephone. I dragged up the front of the filing cabinet and snapped it shut, withdrawing the key. I moved to the door behind Mandrake in time to catch the girl's startled expression when she saw him and tried to connect his appearance with my telephone voice.

"Er—was it you," she asked hesitantly, "that I spoke to on the telephone?"

"No, it was I," I told her, advancing. "Professor Mandrake

just looked in." I brought her into the flat. "I'm Simon Crane," I said, "and this is Professor Mandrake—Miss . . . ?"

"Burton," said the girl rather unhappily, offering a timid hand to the bloodless clasp of the professor. She was small and dark-haired, with a quick, intelligent expression, and wore a dark red linen suit. On the third finger of her left hand glowed an intricate garnet ring. I asked her to sit down and poured her some of my uncle's sherry. She perched on the chair uncertainly, clearly unwilling to bring more limelight than was necessary onto the matter of gramophone records, but impatient to have her hands on the thing and be gone. I could have wished Mandrake elsewhere, but he seemed altogether happy with the situation.

Nobody was helping Miss Burton, so she came to the point herself. "Do you know where they are?" she asked me. "I'm afraid I haven't much time."

"I'm sorry," I said caddishly. "I find, after all, they're locked up. You've had your journey for nothing. I would have told you if I'd known where I could ring you."

She looked deflated, then got to her feet. "I see," she said. "Pity." She smoothed her lapels and squared her shoulders with a defiant gesture. "Oh well," she added. "Another time, no doubt."

"Perhaps if you'd give me your number I could help you," I suggested.

She looked at me half suspiciously. "When will Cyprian be home?"

I felt awful. "Look here," I said. "Sit down a minute, won't you? I should have told you before. My uncle—you see——"

But Mandrake had lost patience with me. "Cyprian's dead," he said bluntly. "He died this afternoon."

She gave a gasp which might have been relief and then the colour left her face. At first I thought she was going to faint, but she only shifted her feet to a firmer stance and stood, guarding her expression, as though she were sifting her emotions before she permitted anything to appear on her face. At last she said quietly, "I shall have to have my record before I go. Please help me."

Of course she had to have her record; far more urgently if he were dead and the record collection about to be split up, inherited or sold, played over by strangers and to strangers, perhaps anyone, perhaps the press. I said, "Yes, of course you must have it," and I started to move towards the cabinet.

Hatred stabbed at me out of her face like an unsheathed knife. "You've played it," she said. I didn't answer. I unlocked the roll-front and let it slide down, took out the records from the tray, selected hers and handed it to her. She took it without a word, looked closely at it, then suspiciously back at me.

"Do you want to make sure?" I asked, glancing over my shoulder at the gramophone. She flashed another look at me, then at Mandrake, clearly not wishing to play it in front of us, and said, "No. I'll go now, if you don't mind."

I opened the door and watched her almost run down the passage.

I turned back into the room. Mandrake was regarding me alertly. "I gather you knew what that was all about?" he suggested, but I didn't answer.

"Now what could there be," he inquired of the air, "in a gramophone record to bring a personable young woman here at this time of day looking as though the devil were one jump behind her? I suppose you hadn't played it?"

"It was something she'd lent him," I answered. "She rang up about it and I promised to find it for her. That's all."

"Don't tell me anything you wouldn't want me to know," said Mandrake in a faintly hurt voice.

"Didn't my uncle ever play you his records?"

"Oh yes. His collection is famous. But this wasn't one of the collection?"

I said, "It appears he made another collection; records he got his women to make for him; love letters, he seems to have called them. I believe he used to play them over to a select few. Did you ever hear those?"

"No, I'm happy to say I didn't," said Mandrake, "though it's perfectly in keeping with my estimate of his character. Have you heard them?"

40

"Yes. They're all from women hopelessly infatuated with him. Obviously intended for no one but himself."

"How do you know anyone else did hear them?"

"From the last one I played. The woman who made that was no fool and she knew him better than the others. She said in it that she was the only one who knew that he played them to give novelty to his parties."

"Do you know who the other women were?" he asked me.

"Of course not," I answered rather quickly. "They're just voices; six women wailing for their demon lover. One of them threatened to kill herself if he didn't come back to her. The horrible thing is that he kept them."

"The amazing thing is that he died an accidental death. More people must have wished him dead than one could readily count, yet he was permitted to die by his own clumsiness in looking out of his own window . . ." Mandrake paused in his speech and his face became furled as though the intelligence had withdrawn elsewhere. "Clumsiness?" he repeated, seeming to examine the word for flaws. "No. It couldn't have been clumsiness. Cyprian wasn't clumsy; neat and nimble as a cat in all his words and actions. Cyprian was precise, pedantic, previous; he touched things with his finger tips; he didn't bump into things with his shoulder. If the window sash were upheld only by a wooden prop, Cyprian would have been aware of it and wary of it."

"Suicide?" I prompted, unconvincingly.

"Would you choose that way to die? Would anyone? Would a man like your uncle take his life and miss the opportunity of leaving an exquisitely worded last note that would make headlines and push up his sales?"

His shapeless features seemed to sharpen to a point, his eyes focusing into greenish specks that would have made me uneasy if they had been boring into me instead of backwards into his own mentality. I had wanted to find out if he knew anything of the girl on the record, but I was sorry now that I had said so much. Playing for time, I answered, "You knew him better than I."

"So I did," he agreed, "and on that knowledge I'll say no, he wouldn't kill himself like that; and I don't believe he would die accidentally like that, either."

He was looking into me now and not into himself any more, until his gaze became unbearable. Feeling absurdly guilty, I dropped my eyes. "What made you play those records before you'd been in the house an hour?" he asked.

"Well, actually it was because the girl rang up and wanted to come over and get hers. She sounded so agitated. I wondered, just as you did, why a record should so concern her. And when I couldn't unlock the cabinet I got curious."

"Wasn't there a key?"

"Yes, it was on my uncle's key ring."

"But it didn't unlock the cabinet?" he asked searchingly. "Why not?"

"There was something in the lock."

"What?"

"A bit of wire."

Mandrake held out his hand, and with no volition of my own, I dropped the twisted hairpin into his palm. He grunted twice, turned it over, and then his eyes bored back into mine. The friendly, rather clumsily shy personality with whom I had spent the evening had vanished and here was a steel-hard intellect with eyes that could not be deceived. Mandrake held out his hand. "What else?" he said.

Shamefacedly, like a boy caught playing truant, I handed over the bit of torn paper and the crystal earring, and permitted him to drag out of me where and how I had found them. He took a clean envelope from the rack on the desk and dropped them into it. Then he turned back to me. "And the police," he boomed suddenly in my ear, "were they still satisfied it was an accident after you'd told them?"

"I didn't tell them," I stammered.

"Didn't tell the police?" he repeated incredulously.

"I didn't find anything till after they'd made their examination and left the flat."

He rose to his feet and loomed over me like a doom. "You

mean to tell me you've had this information in your hands since—what time?"

"About seven o'clock, I suppose."

"Since seven o'clock, and now it's nearly midnight, and you haven't mentioned it to a soul except me?"

"No one," I said.

The lowering features were suddenly lit by a smile of utter delight. "But how perfectly wonderful," said Mandrake. "I'd almost given up hoping that something like this could happen to me."

I gazed at him openmouthed, as, with an expression of the most innocent happiness, he unsheathed his fountain pen, helped himself to a sheet of Cyprian's paper, drew it towards him and wrote boldly across the top, "*New Statesman* Murder —first draft." Then underneath, spacing the words down the page so that he could fill in the gaps later, he wrote, "Time, Clues, Suspects, Motives." He thought for a minute, added the word "Hunches," then drew back and smiled apologetically. "There's one thing I feel I ought to mention right away," he said. "You talk too much. If we don't keep this thing absolutely to ourselves we shall have people getting suspicious and interfering and calling in the police. Now the very first thing you did was to tell me everything you knew."

"I didn't intend to," I protested.

"Precisely. Without meaning to in the least, you told everything you knew to the first person who made a determined effort to get at the facts. That sort of thing won't do at all, now will it?"

"I suppose not," I replied weakly.

"I might have had very good reasons for wanting to find out just how much you suspected. I might be Cyprian's murderer myself."

"But surely everything points to a woman?"

"You can't be certain of anything. *I'm* a keen reader of the *New Statesman*. I could have planted the earring as a blind. I've got no alibi for this afternoon."

"I see what you mean," I answered, beginning to enter into

43

the thing, and entirely willing to draw the scent further away from the voice that I personally suspected. "It was the hairpin that I had in mind, but come to think of it, plenty of men might carry a hairpin for one reason or another. To clean a pipe, for instance, or . . ."

"For something like this?" suggested Mandrake, sliding a thumb behind his lapel and turning it, with its buttonhole forward, so that I saw that the stem of the flower had been secured to the lapel by a small, bent silver hairpin.

"So you see," said Mandrake severely but not unkindly, as he turned the lapel back into place, "you really can't be too careful to whom you talk."

CHAPTER FOUR

"And now," said Mandrake, with his fountain pen once more poised over the paper, "we must establish the time at which death occurred."

"The doctor said approximately four o'clock," I answered.

"At any rate, it was some time before you arrived and the manager opened up the flat. When was that?"

"Six," I replied. "And we know he was alive at half-past two when Brady left."

Mandrake jotted on the paper under "Time" and then paused at "Clues."

"An earring," he murmured, "a hairpin and a torn scrap of the *New Statesman*. Now here"—he leaned back and his intelligence seemed to draw off and hover—"we are handling something that could give us a definite approach to the mentality of the murderer. The fact that he read the *New Statesman* rules out quite a number of types which one would normally associate with murder. Such a person would be very unlikely to commit a crime of passion; on the other hand, he or she would be more likely to do murder for an idea than the average man or woman."

"Only one can't be certain," I suggested, "that the murderer was a regular reader. He might have bought it at a bookstall, for want of something better."

"No," said Mandrake. "One would as soon buy a publication of the wrong political or religious view. People buy the *New Statesman* on purpose or not at all. We can assume that the murderer belongs to an intelligent minority, tolerant of everything except intolerance and complacency; and thanking God that he or she is not as other men. I take the *New Statesman* myself," he added helpfully.

He added a few words under his heading of "Suspects" and then asked, "Is there anything to suggest that anyone entered the flat between Brady's departure at half-past two and your arrival at six?"

"According to Brady, he wasn't expecting anyone, and Mrs. Best from the flat directly underneath said she didn't hear anyone enter the flat during the afternoon."

"Would she have heard, do you suppose?"

"There's nothing above *this* flat but the roof, so it's hard to judge how much one can hear. Of course the manager said they were all soundproof, but I got the impression that was pure wishful thinking."

"Why?"

"Mrs. Best said Cyprian had been playing his gramophone all morning."

Mandrake's gaze sharpened. "Did she say what he'd been playing?"

"Yes, as it happens, she did. Ravel's *Daphnis and Chloë.*"

"And were those particular records in the cabinet when you opened it, or were they somewhere else in the flat?"

"They were all in the cabinet," I told him.

"I see," said Mandrake. "Then the attempt to pick the lock was made today, after he had replaced them, since he couldn't

45

have closed and locked the cabinet while that piece of hairpin was there. And since Cyprian never left the flat all day, and the lock can hardly have been picked in his presence, it was done after he was dead and before your arrival. I think we can assume that the cabinet contains either the motive for the murder or else something that would focus suspicion on the murderer. Wouldn't it be as well for us to play the remaining records?"

But whatever else happened, I did not intend that he should hear them. "Not tonight," I said, getting to my feet. "I'm sorry, but I've had a long day and now it's after midnight. I'm going to bed."

His face was pathetic but he took it well. "I suppose you're right," he said. "Oh dear, and tomorrow's Saturday. I'm all tied up lecturing to schoolboys."

"Too bad," I said. "And I'm tied up all of Sunday."

"If only we'd got onto this earlier in the evening we needn't have wasted so much time. Could you lunch on Monday?"

But I was to lunch with Anstey from my firm's London office on Monday.

"Never mind," said Mandrake. "I'll think of something and ring you. Here's my number, in case anything fresh turns up." He had folded his paper and put it in his breast pocket and was almost at the door before I reminded him that he'd still got the envelope with the clues in it.

"So I have," he said, trying to look surprised. "You will take care of them, won't you?" He put the envelope in my hand. The uncouth, ungainly figure paused a moment in the doorway, gave me a wistful smile of extraordinary charm and padded away down the passage.

I lay awake a long time and then slept late into the morning. I was awakened by Brady with a breakfast tray and a couple of newspapers, neither of which was the *Recorder*. I breakfasted sparsely on the thin toast, honey and prunes which appeared to be habitual with my uncle, then dressed and moved into the study which Brady was in process of "doing." As I watched him brushing and Hoovering the carpets and chairs, delving with scrupulous industry into the crannies of chairs and settee, I realised that no unauthorised bauble could survive his scrutiny. The earring on the settee could not have been there the previous morning. It must have got there later in the day, and, as Brady had been certain no visitor had been there before he left at half-past two, it could only have arrived after that and before we found my uncle.

Brady hadn't a manner that invited questions, but I was curious about so much that I had to talk to him.

"What used to happen to my uncle's manuscripts?" I asked. "Apart from the portable typewriter, I've never seen a room so innocent of any evidence of writing."

"Mr. Druse never kept anything after it had been published," Brady explained, "and the thing he had been working on recently has just gone to the typist."

"He didn't do his own typing, then?"

"Good gracious, no; he used that machine very rarely. His articles for the *Sunday Reviewer* and so forth were delivered in longhand, and I took the manuscript of his new book to Miss Tangent about a fortnight ago. There is nothing else."

"Not even a box of rejects somewhere in a cupboard?"

"Rejects, sir?" Brady could never have heard the word before.

I explained about rejected manuscripts.

"Oh no," said Brady. "Mr. Druse hadn't any of those."

Outside agency hours I was a free-lance myself; only in a very small way, but, yes, I knew about rejects. Smarting a little, I said, "Of course Mr. Druse's output was unusually small and most of his work was commissioned."

"As you say, sir," agreed Brady, easing out a bookcase so that he might dust the skirting behind it with almost morbid thoroughness. I began to weary of him. "Would you get me a *Daily Recorder*?" I asked.

"Mr. Druse had *The Times* and the *News Chronicle* delivered every day," he assured me.

"But it's the *Recorder* I would like," I explained sunnily. "Would you go out and get me one before they're sold out?"

I was curious to know if the paragraph incorrectly reporting my inheritance of Cyprian's records had appeared, and I wanted to play the record from the cabinet over again.

Brady collected his cleaning apparatus and retired and was no sooner out of the flat than the door buzzer sounded.

My heart started to beat wildly. If I could not control it at this stage, how could I hope to handle the interview so that I learned anything and came out the victor? In any case, I told myself, it wouldn't be her—couldn't be her, yet.

It wasn't. At first I thought it was a child and then I realised it was a slight, rather haggard woman with a tangle of fair hair and a dirndl dress. Her face was lit with a too-ecstatic frenzy of recognition which I felt to be misplaced. But no. "Mr. Crane," she said, "I'm Mrs. Best. I was here when you came. *You* know." And welcoming warmth ran all over her face, assurance that *now* I should be equally delighted. I felt that she had been trying the expression on her face all the way up from her flat. She held a bottle of Grade A milk.

"I've brought you some milk," she said, stepping past me into the flat. "It's what you'll need. I don't suppose you were able to eat a thing yesterday after the shock. You should drink it hot."

She was in the kitchen selecting a saucepan by now. I had been right about her. This was certainly the woman whose recorded voice bore my uncle's label of "The Sacred Cow." Permitting my pale protests that I had supped heartily and had but just eaten a sizable breakfast to fall about her like unregarded hail, she continued, "Men don't take care of themselves unless someone makes them. Especially creative men. Poor Cyprian was just the same. Poor doomed Cyprian. If he would have listened, what I could have saved him. But men won't. Not men like that with greatness eating them. He followed his destiny. His brain wore out his body."

"Actually," I answered rather crisply, for it was much too early in the morning with me for this sort of conversation, "it was the window sash wore out his vertebrae."

48

She gave me a look. "Ah," she said, "you're like me. You don't *show* things. You *feel* things—here." Without looking I knew that her hand was pressed to her ribs to the left of her thorax. "You must have thought me terribly callous last evening," she went on, "when we found—*him*." Her eyes drilled into me, sizing up the effect she was making. "How could I show my real feelings in front of *them*? How could I permit our exquisite relationship to be dragged in the dust and assessed on that plane which those men inhabit?"

The milk started to boil over and it became clear that Mrs. Best could operate in both planes at once, for she snatched it from the stove and had it inclined over the beaker before it had foamed to the top of the pan. She stood the pan under the cold tap in the sink, placed the beaker on a saucer, handed it to me and led me back into the study.

"You must relax; sit down while you drink it, and put your feet up whenever you can."

I said, "Yes, it would be heartbreaking if I dropped it at seven months," but she refused to acknowledge that I had made any remark at all.

"I know so much better than you," she persisted, "what a shock of that type means to a sensitive nature."

I had no idea what had convinced her of my intense sensitiveness and I wasn't able to feel very curious. She was a fake and my uncle had known it, presumably permitting her to make a fool of herself to the top of her bent on the record for whatever dubious entertainment it might afford him. Admittedly, if she had used a hairpin, the silvery one that had picked the lock would be a likely enough colour, but I couldn't imagine that yellowish tangle confined by anything so definite as a style requiring pins. The earring, too, she might have worn, though I would have expected something more flamboyant. She lived close enough, certainly, and wished me to suppose that she had been on intimate terms with my uncle, but nothing would induce me to believe she had had any hand in his death. For one thing, she had no motive, for I couldn't suppose that she minded having made the record in the least.

But it was not even safe to pursue my train of thought, for "You're thinking too much," she said suddenly. "You ought to relax while you drink your milk."

The man who could have relaxed under that gaze of fixed expectancy would have been at ease in a tiger's cage.

"I can't relax to order," I protested, but of course this was something she could "understand," too.

"I'm just the same," she said. "It was worse yesterday. Even before I *knew*. The feeling of tension; it came over me in the fish queue. And then when I got home; the glove—everything; it was as though I'd lived through it all before."

I pricked up my ears. "You had a feeling in the fish queue *before* you knew Cyprian was dead?" I asked.

"Oh yes. Like a pall; a sense of deep personal loss. I can't describe it."

"Yesterday morning," I asked, "or afternoon?"

"It was in the afternoon," she said. "It didn't look fresh in the morning."

"So that feeling you had in the fish queue must have coincided exactly with Cyprian's death, mustn't it?"

"It must have," she agreed, in a hush of wonder at her own psychic capacities.

"The doctor said he must have died at about four o'clock."

"Yes—yes," she pondered delightedly. "I left home about twenty past three to change my library book and stopped for the fish on my way back. It must have been quite four before I left the shop. How extraordinary."

She was spellbound by this new light on her possibilities, but I was more concerned with the realisation that she couldn't have been in the flat below at the time when Cyprian's murderer must have come and gone, and that her statement to the police that she heard no one above was worth even less consideration than I had given it.

"So you must have found the blood on your glove almost as soon as you got home?"

"Oh no," she answered. "I washed the gloves when I got home and then had tea. I'd been sitting over tea about an hour

50

before I noticed the drop of blood. I can't *tell* you what I felt like."

But of course she did. I was wondering if anyone else had been near enough to the flat to have heard a visitor, but it was no use asking her. I didn't suppose for one moment she had deliberately withheld from the police the fact that she hadn't been at home at the exact time. It was simply that she couldn't bear to be out of the picture. I felt sure that, once the suggestion of murder had crossed her mind, she would invent evidence rather than admit she knew nothing.

I said, "I hope the gramophone isn't an awful nuisance," and that was right down her street. "Oh no. How could it be?" she asked. "Cyprian's wonderful music. I simply drank it in."

"Flats are never quite as soundproof as the advertisements suggest, are they?" I asked.

She smilingly agreed. "Not that Cyprian made much noise," she added, "but we always knew whether he was there or not."

"I suppose you knew a good many of his friends?" I hazarded, supposing nothing of the sort, but wondering if she could tell me anything about one particular woman. Her face fell a little. "Not really, no, not many." Then she rallied. "Cyprian knew I didn't care for parties."

I felt sure that there was nothing more she could tell me, but she still chattered happily and made no move to go, so I asked her if by chance she could lend me the week's *New Statesman*, hoping she would offer to fetch me her copy, and once I had got her out of the flat I could have seen to it that she stayed out. Mrs. Best, however, had never heard of that publication. As I racked my brain for another exit cue, the telephone rang. I snatched off the receiver but it was only Anstey from the London office. Better than nothing, however, in the circumstances. I put my hand over the receiver and turned to her apologetically. "I'm afraid this will keep me a longish time," I said, "so perhaps . . ."

Reluctantly she withdrew.

Anstey was full of concern for my situation and offered to put me up until I could get into an hotel. The booking he had arranged for me at the Park Lane wasn't for another fortnight and he hadn't been able to put it forward. London was crowded like everywhere else, and he'd drawn a blank so far with the other hotels. I assured him that I was all right where I was for the present. He seemed relieved, and reminded me that we were lunching on Monday and dining at the Critics' Group dinner in the evening, where there would be several people I should find it useful to meet. I then telephoned the management of the flats to find out the name of Cyprian's solicitor, and rang him up to tell him what had happened. Before I rang off the door buzzer went, and Brady, returning with my newspaper, asked if I would see a Mr. Condor.

Mr. Condor was young, well-brought-up and in a state of nervous tension. He asked to see some of my uncle's records with a view to purchase. I explained that they were not mine. He produced the *Daily Recorder* and showed me the gossip paragraph which had appeared that morning. I assured him it must be a mistake. He turned rather pale and ran his finger inside his collar. He was sorry, he said, but he'd come a long way and it was urgent. There was a record in the collection which he had to have. I told him I could do nothing and offered him the address of Cyprian's solicitor. His face grew frantic and just then the door buzzer went again. Brady told me another gentleman was asking for me. I went to the door.

It was the coroner's officer to take depositions and see the body. He had already interviewed Mrs. Best, the porter and a member of the firm of builders who might be held, to some extent, responsible. I told him everything the police knew already and nothing that they didn't. He said the inquest would probably be on Monday and offered to arrange for an undertaker to take the body away if I liked. I did like. When I returned the study was upside down, with every drawer open and books pulled off the shelves. Mr. Condor was ransacking the room and scarcely seemed to care whether I was present or not.

"I wouldn't do that if I were you," I suggested, but he only answered, "Oh yes, you would," and went on with his search.

"Look here," I said quite reasonably, "I'm bigger than you and in wonderful condition. Suppose you tell me what you're up to while you still can. Maybe I can help."

He looked at me once. "Would you if you could?" he asked.

"If you had a good enough reason."

"You're Druse's nephew," he stated, as though that precluded my being a human being.

"I am," I agreed, "but I never met him. *You* tell me."

"Death was too good for him," said Condor.

"You just put the room tidy," I suggested, "and relax and tell me about it. I'm listening."

He looked at me suspiciously. "You don't write for the papers or anything?" he asked.

I assured him I didn't, and started putting the books back on the shelves. Condor's eye fell on the filing cabinet and he leapt towards it.

"Yes, they're in that cabinet," I said. "Why is it so important to you?"

I had to twist his arm behind him or I think he would have torn the cabinet apart. Gasping for breath, he said, "I've got to have that record."

"What record?" I asked.

"My sister made it."

"Your sister is a musician?"

"Of course not. It's not one of those. Just a homemade voice recording. Means nothing in the world to anyone but my sister."

"Who is your sister?"

"Oh, no one in particular from your point of view. If you've got to know, she was in love with this uncle of yours. Made a fool of herself and then tried to kill herself."

"When?"

"About eighteen months ago. I found her. She wouldn't tell me much, just wanted to be left alone to die. She was ill for months and I thought she'd go out of her mind, but she didn't. In fact, she met a decent chap who fell in love with her and they were married last month."

"What was his name?" I asked, but he ignored me and went on, "She came round to me first thing this morning as I was leaving for the office. She looked terrible—like she'd looked the day I'd found her. She showed me this paragraph and told me she'd made a record and sent it to him when he'd got tired of her—a sort of last appeal, saying she'd wait three days for him to answer and if he didn't, she'd kill herself."

I had to let go of his arm and he gave a sort of groan and covered his face with his hands. "He *did* answer," he went on in a flat, bitter voice; "he sent her a card, thanking her for her present and saying it would make a valuable addition to his collection."

"Good God!" I gasped.

"So she knew he'd kept it with his others, and she said that if the collection were sold and anyone got hold of her record there'd be a news story in it and it would get in the papers and then she'd kill herself. So I've got to get it."

"People who say they'll commit suicide never mean it," I said unconvincingly.

"She does," said Condor. "Be reasonable. If there's any rap to come, I'll take it. Just turn your back or leave me alone in the room till I've destroyed it. No one else will ever know that it existed. You can't stand by and let her kill herself."

I supposed I couldn't. I realised I had overestimated my powers of resistance when I invented the paragraph. On the other hand, if anyone had good reason to welcome Cyprian's death, this man's sister had. Suppose she had killed him and failed to find her record, mightn't her brother be behaving in precisely this way? Once I had parted with the record I had no way of checking on either of them, and the chances were that he hadn't even given me his real name.

"Look here," I said, "if you'll trust me a little more, I'll trust you. Take me to meet your sister, and if I'm satisfied, you can come back here with me and I'll give you the record."

He considered the proposition. "All right," he said. "I'll take you to meet her, but only if you bring the record with you."

"Very well," I agreed. "And now suppose you wait in the passage till I've packed it up?"

He looked disappointed, but permitted me to lead him outside the flat and to close the door in his face. I selected the record which bore Cyprian's pencilled note "She didn't die, though" and put it into a leather dispatch case that was in the desk drawer. Then I locked the cabinet and told Brady not to leave the flat or to admit anyone till I returned.

In the street I suggested a taxi, but Condor said we should never get one and when I pointed out an empty one, cruising, he said, "It'll only take a minute."

He led me through bustling crowds and across streets busy with traffic, talking so wildly and incoherently that I knew exactly what was in his mind and was prepared for it when he turned, made a sudden grab for the dispatch case and tried to dart off through the traffic. My foot was round his ankle and he was sprawling across the pavement with the dispatch case skidding under a dray horse's hoofs. I retrieved the case before helping to dust him off, then, with a firm grip on his wrist, I led him down the steps of an underground station and parked the case in the cloakroom. I put the ticket in my trousers pocket.

"Come along," I said, "let's go and see your sister."

CHAPTER FIVE

It took longer than I had anticipated. His sister lived at Notting Hill in a little house in a row. She had mouse-brown hair, a round, soft face which should have been plump and round blue eyes which should have been limpid and unshadowed but which were haunted and darting and afraid. Her husband was an earnest young civil servant, clearly in the process of trying to understand her. They welcomed us with startled looks, and Condor—whose name proved to be Ratcliffe—introduced me and explained that we just happened to be passing on our way to, I think, Shepherd's Bush, and he thought he'd look in to welcome them home. They offered us tea, beer, or poached eggs if we could stay so long, but it appeared we were lunching at Shepherd's Bush. Mrs. Creel, the sister, could only stare at me with fascinated dread while her husband apologised for the untidiness of the room, explaining that they had returned from their honeymoon in Perthshire late on the previous evening and were in process of unpacking. I realised then that there were half-empty cases on the floor and that piles of assorted clothing reposed on most of the furniture.

That was all the alibi she needed. She couldn't have been with Cyprian when he died. I apologised for arriving at such an awkward moment, said "O.K." to the brother, shook hands and started for the door with Creel showing me out. I held him in conversation just long enough for Ratcliffe to reassure his sister. Then we headed for the underground station where I gave him the record and parted from him without rancour.

They had just arrived for the body when I got back, and as soon as it was off the premises Brady told me that Professor Mandrake had been on the telephone and had left a message that I was to look in the *Recorder*, page three. I knew very well by now that my gossip paragraph had appeared, but I didn't expect to find on page three the photograph of the actress who had called the previous evening, beside a prosperous, heavily built young man. The picture was captioned, "The engagement was announced yesterday of Janet Drury, now appearing in *Bedrock* at the St. Martin's, and Paul Cleveland, son of Horace Cleveland of the Cleveland House Coffee Company."

Paul Cleveland looked as though the coffee company was quite a good thing and his bride-to-be looked innocent and adoring. No, she'd scarcely want her record to crop up at this stage in her existence, and you could hardly blame her for giving me the wrong name. But I was certain the amazement on her face at the news of his death was genuine, and that she had come merely believing that my uncle was away and taking the opportunity to try and retrieve her record for her own sake.

So now I had met three of the voices, and even been as far as Notting Hill just to make certain of the thing I was certain of already. Not one of them had done it. As for the remaining three voices, there was nothing whatever to suggest any motive for the Lisle Street one, and I felt I could count her out of the running. That left only the poetess, Cynthia Spalding, and the sixth, unidentified voice. I felt sure that she would identify herself in some way before the sun went down.

By next morning I almost began to wonder if I had mistaken my woman. There was still no sign of her. It was Sunday and, having told Brady I shouldn't need him, I got my own breakfast and then made my bed and even dusted the more noticeably polished surfaces in the flat. If she came I meant to be ready.

Every minute I felt so certain she would come that I couldn't bring myself to leave the flat. I rang down to the restaurant and told them to send up lunch which I ate in solitude by the open window. Even the sunshine could not dispel a queer consciousness of my uncle about the place nor of his murderer, who might be anywhere but who was surely on her way to me by now.

Only once the telephone shrilled through the silence, and then it was Mandrake, who said he was tied up with guests and couldn't get away but suggested I come over and spend the evening with them. I told him I too was tied up and couldn't get away.

I prowled the flat, dipping into my uncle's first editions, rereading some of his own publications, even unearthing the volume of Cynthia Spalding's verse which contained *Immaculate Despoiler,* and finding it very much better work than my uncle's review had led me to expect. In the end I always came back to the gramophone. Dusk found me morbidly hunched in a chair, with my eyes shut and the record playing, trying to put a face and form onto that disturbing voice that had filled my heart and emptied my head of any useful endeavour.

As it got to the middle for the third time, the telephone smashed into the queer dark intimacy of the voice. I snatched off the sound arm and lifted the receiver.

"Simon Crane?"

My heart began to thump. You couldn't be as sure as that on two words; all the same, I was sure. I thanked God for every time I had resisted the impulse to go out during that long, lonely day. The silence sung between us, alive with tension. "Speaking," I said.

"You wouldn't know me." The voice came again, deep, lazy indifferent. What was it to her that I would know her voice anywhere; in the dark, in the tomb, in the chorus of the *Little Revue,* if I should chance to hear it in those places? I said: "What can I do for you?"

"Well, I wondered if you could spare me a few minutes? It's rather urgent and I'd prefer not to explain over the telephone. I'm afraid it sounds a little odd, but you'll understand everything when I tell you . . ."

"But certainly," I assured her. "Come on over to the flat. I'll be pouring you out a sherry."

"Oh, thank you, no. I didn't mean that. I'm in the little Green Bar in your building, beyond the swimming pool, and I can't leave because I'm expecting someone else. I thought if you could join me for a drink before they come, it would be so simple . . ."

It wasn't fair. She had to come to the flat and she had to come alone. I said, "But I prefer my encounters complicated."

"Don't worry." The voice was penetratingly, disturbingly intimate. "This one will be complicated in the extreme. Shall I expect you?"

It was scarcely even an inquiry. This woman knew that men came when she asked them, where she asked them.

"Wait a moment," I protested. "I'm not sure I can get away. And if I can, how am I to know you?"

"You won't need to," the voice said slowly. *"I shall know you."* And she rang off.

The whole elaborately laid scheme was out of my control already just because a sleepy-voiced woman had said, "Shall I expect you?" I should be there and she knew it—and the encounter was to be "complicated in the extreme." Yes, I thought ruefully, complicated by the presence of that other person for whom she was waiting and the barmen and all the assortment of people who frequented the cocktail bar. What hope had I of finding out anything at all about her in those surroundings? No, I must keep my advantage and not turn up. If it were as important to her as this, she wouldn't let that discourage her. She would try again, and when I refused to meet her anywhere else she would have to accept my terms and come to the flat.

Only while I was expounding to myself this very reasonable theory, I was brushing my hair and polishing my shoes. It was not till I got to the door that I remembered the gramophone record was still on the turntable.

After all, with any luck I might bring her back to the flat, for her record was here and she surely meant to have it, and that was one thing she wouldn't do without coming to the flat and giving a very good account of herself. In fact, I should be very foolish not to meet her now that I had the chance. It was the most reasonable thing to do.

But it wouldn't do for her to find her record on the gramophone. I might wish her to suppose I'd never played any of the records and was entirely ignorant of their content. I lifted it from the turntable and put it flat on the top of the wardrobe in my bedroom. Then I let myself out and hurried across the courtyard of Pendervil Mansions to my rendezvous.

I found that the front block of the buildings had flats only on the upper floors, the rest of it consisting of a swimming pool, squash courts, a restaurant, a row of small, shuttered shops, an American bar, a Crush Bar and the Green Bar. The Green Bar was the smallest, shrillest and clearly the most expensive. Stools, tables, bar and all the fittings were made of some substance which appeared to be green glass but which probably wasn't. Not a stool nor a bit of leaning space was vacant. The place was packed with the smartest people I had seen since I landed in England, and, at a casual glance, the nastiest.

It was the last sort of gathering I had ever wished to be a part of, but *she* was part of it; so unobtrusively a part of it that I could not even separate anyone from the rest that I could imagine being the owner of her voice. She had said, "*I* shall know *you.*" How that could be possible I could not imagine. Except for my jaunt to Notting Hill, I had not set foot outside the flat since my arrival. Could she have seen my arrival, I wondered, could she have somehow been watching the flats when I went out? It was impossible to conjecture. Next moment, no doubt, that sleepy, intimate voice would speak my name, and there would be a face to the voice that could never be a stranger's face to me, who knew so much about her.

I shifted from foot to foot. No one stepped up to greet me. No voice spoke my name out of the hubbub. Hard London faces turned to regard me for a second, then flicked me off as they flicked off the ash from their cigarettes. Still I waited, feeling out of it and absurd and becoming aware that my shoes squeaked a little. Three women pushed past me, and one of them, who was jangling with horrible Art jewellery, spoke in a whisper, and then the three of them laughed. None of them could have been she, nor could they have been laughing at me, but I blushed suddenly scarlet and turned and strode through the exit, squeaking a little in my good new shoes. I went back across the courtyard and up in the lift, but it was not till I let myself in that I realised how willingly I had taken the bait. For you can tell, as you go into an apartment, if there has been someone recently in it. A faint feeling of warmth, an air of occupancy. No living person was in the flat now, I quickly ascertained, but faint on the air was perfume that had not been there when I left. And the records in the shelf of the cabinet marked "These I have loved" were gone.

One of the drawers in my room was not quite shut and a bit of my sock was sticking out of it. My suitcases had been opened too. But when I groped with my fingers along the top of the wardrobe, the record was safe. I felt better. I had been fooled, but I still held the card. She would have to come back.

I began to wonder how in thunder she'd got in, and just what, if it was so easy, was going to prevent her from murdering me in my sleep. Oh well, I could probably prevent her myself if it became necessary. I was six foot two and in possession of my health and strength, even if I did wear squeaky shoes. It wasn't my skin that I was afraid for anyway, but my heart and my head and, a little, my sense of humour.

I went through the flat systematically but could not find that any of the doors or windows were negotiable. I was beginning to believe that she must possess a key to the flat, when, going into the kitchen, I noticed what should have been obvious to a half-wit all the time. The kitchen was built on an inside wall and depended both for light and ventilation on a skylight, operated by a rope pulley and reached by a short metal fire-escape ladder, flat against the wall behind the door. As the door had always been open when I was in the room, it had hidden the ladder from view. Now I ascended it quickly and found that the window, though open only a few inches, could easily be pulled wider by any enterprising person on the roof. I pushed out my head and shoulders and looked at the vista of roofs in the London night. I climbed out and found that the roofs were flat, marked off at intervals by low division walls, that most of the flats had similar skylights and some boasted elaborate roof gardens. At the corner there was an exterior fire escape, running down as far as the fourth floor, where it was received by a sort of parapet and disappeared inside the building. I climbed over the intervening walls and made my way down the escape till I was back in the building, but I found no one there. I came back up the staircase and let myself in again. Then I made the rope pulley properly fast and went to bed.

I awakened next morning before Brady arrived and, feeling certain that he would dust the top of the wardrobe, I retrieved the record, wrapped it in brown paper and found a new hiding place behind the kitchen cabinet. During breakfast Brady and I were notified that the inquest would be held at eleven-thirty, and that we should both be required to attend. I got the impression that attending inquests had not been part of his duties in Brady's previous situations. When he had cleared away, Mrs. Best's brown-haired little sister Hazel called. I opened the door.

"Hullo," she said. "I'm only Myrtle Best's sister. Sorry to bother you."

"No bother at all," I said. "I knew I'd met you somewhere," and stood aside for her to come in. As she came in she said, "No, you haven't met me."

"I suppose we must have passed on the stairs."

"Not even that," she said. "I'm just such an ordinary type that everyone thinks they've met me and didn't remember. Or else when they have they don't. You'll probably walk past me tomorrow. Did my sister leave a milk bottle?"

"I don't know. Yes, I suppose she did. Do you want it?"

"Not personally, but the milkman's raising hell. Myrtle's always doing it. Gets extra milk from him by looking as though she'd drop to pieces in a brisk wind, then she dumps it on any misunderstood genius she runs into and the milkman never gets the bottle back. You'll know it because it's got Express on it. Yours is the Co-op."

She had led the way into the kitchen by now, clearly to Brady's disgust, and was hunting high and low for the alien bottle, which she ran to earth under the sink. She rinsed it, wiped it firmly on a cloth and returned with me as far as the passage. I said, "Won't you come in for a minute?"

"I don't have to," she answered. "I fancy my sister's made enough running for me to give you a miss."

I steered her into the study. "She makes such a fool of herself," said my visitor, "that I've had to adopt this brisk, businesslike attitude in self-defence. Tell me if it's beginning to pall."

"It isn't yet," I assured her. "But I'd be grateful if you could convince your sister that I'm neither misunderstood nor a genius."

"It's a terrible strain, isn't it," she agreed, "I'm her unsought-after little sister Hazel with no sex appeal. I've got to be found a man. That's quite nerve-racking too, in its quiet way."

I offered her a cigarette, which she refused. "I'd no idea there was anyone but Mrs. Best in the flat below," I said.

"I'm only up for a fortnight. More than a week's gone already and I'm still unclaimed. She'll have to work fast."

"Were you in the fish queue with her on Friday?" I asked suddenly.

She looked a bit startled. "On Friday, no. Why Friday?"

"The day I arrived."

"Oh yes. The day your uncle . . . yes, of course. No. I was downstairs washing my hair. Why?"

"Why didn't you come up with the others?"

"Well, for one thing, my hair was still wet, and for another, I don't take an all that passionate interest in other people's affairs."

"Not when they so far forget themselves as to drip blood on your window sill?"

"Look here, I'm sorry, but as a matter of fact, your uncle and all his doings just aren't my cup of tea. I'd seen him a couple of times in the lift but I thought he looked The End. Myrtle was perfectly silly about him, and I always try to steer clear of the people she makes a fool of herself over. I'm on the defensive with them all the time, like I am with you. For all I knew, he and his buddy were probably just doing something nasty with goat's blood or chicken's gall, and that drop of blood was just what I'd been expecting for days. When Myrtle went off with the glove to reconnoitre, I was very happy to stay out of it."

"You said 'he and his buddy'; was there someone with him?"

"Well, I'd heard the door buzzer earlier in the afternoon, and then his voice and a woman's, I think. His window was open, you know, and so was ours. I don't know when she left. You don't hear anything while you're washing your hair. But it was a long time after that that my sister noticed the blood."

She looked as though she might be thinking, and I couldn't feel that anything useful could come of any more people thinking, so I said, "Had you any reason to suppose he dabbled in black magic?"

"Good lord, no," she replied. "I just thought he was nasty enough for anything. Sorry about him being your uncle."

"Oh, that's all right," I assured her. "It's rather refreshing to come across a woman who wasn't fascinated by him."

"Yes, that's what I am, refreshing. Enjoy it while it's new. It palls in no time at all."

"You're a singularly bitter young woman."

"It's palling already. I'll take my bottle and go. We've got one outstayer of welcomes in our family already."

She was at the door.

I said, "I hope you come back sometime. Don't wait till there's a bottle to round up."

"That's rather nice of you," she said, stopping with her hand on the knob to smile, for the first time since I'd seen her. "I'll try not to presume on it," and she went.

Brady and I then left for the inquest, where the coroner brought in a verdict of Death by Misadventure.

At one I met Anstey, who took me to lunch at the Caprice, where everyone seemed to know everyone else but me. Quite a number knew Anstey, however, and they couldn't have been nicer to me, once they realised that I had just come from Cyprian's inquest and that I'd actually seen the body. Anstey, who had seemed rather gloomy about my uncle's untimely end, began to realise that he was probably going to be almost as helpful to us dead as he would have been alive.

I went back with him to the London office to meet the other members of the firm and then returned to the flat in time to dress for the Critics' Group dinner.

My trunk had arrived and Brady had unpacked it and was pressing my evening suit. I shed my squeaky shoes gratefully and propped Cyprian's bedroom open while I bathed and dressed, so that I should not any more be assailed by the uneasy suspicion that he was still there, but even so his presence never left the flat.

The Critics' Group dinner was much as I had expected, with a number of flamboyantly literary types, a sprinkling of stage celebrities, a very successful female writer of domestic comedies and the small fry from most of the literary agencies round an inconspicuous nucleus of actual critics.

Anstey identified the principal figures in the room for me as we dined. Presently there were toasts and speeches, and into every speech my uncle's presence, or rather, absence, intruded. Not one of the speakers felt able to sit down without paying some sort of tribute to the memory of Cyprian Druse. The critics proper spoke of the loss to their profession of one of the few remaining figures of any genuine stature; a leading actor said that on opening his *Sunday Reviewer* and not finding the customary article, he would feel as though a familiar face had gone—but he did not say a friend. The female playwright was the only one who came anything like out into the open, when she admitted that she would feel safer in future, since she well knew hers was the type of playwriting which, above all others, he detested, but added untruthfully that she would certainly miss being pilloried in such stimulating fashion. I could not but suspect that the general feeling was of restrained but undeniable relief.

The toastmaster now called upon Marcia Garnett, cinema critic for the *Sunday Reviewer,* and a woman stood up. In this gathering, where most of the women's clothes had attempted too much and achieved too little, she was remarkable for scarcely seeming to have tried at all and for succeeding superbly. She wore a long suit of fine black cloth, cut no more obtrusively well than a man's evening suit, but certainly no less. At her throat and wrists there were small, crisp ruffles of ice blue. Her hair seemed to curl by its own power, carelessly round her head, and looked casual, as though you might run your fingers through it, but I dare swear nobody ever had, twice. It was the exact colour and texture of spun glass. Her eyes were as blue as the ruffles. Her hands were flawlessly groomed but the nails were untinted, and her whole air was of careless perfection for which no one seemed to have tried. But someone had tried. No one ever arrived at that perfection of line and cut and colour entirely by accident. The nose was short, the upper lip short, the ears ivory under the spun-glass hair; the one thing that slipped the frame and disturbed the whole balance of the picture was the wide, warm, velvety mouth. It was a generous mouth, a mouth willing to laugh or cry with you, and it was tinted a deep petunia which exactly repeated the colour of the flower clamped with a diamond clip to her lapel. Oh, certainly someone had tried.

Here was a woman who might have moved over her sisters' heads in almost any line of country which demanded poise, beauty or any of the feminine attributes, yet she had deliberately thrown these advantages away and chosen to compete with her wit and intelligence in a literary career and still had got to the top. She must be dynamite, I thought. She must be invincible. But when she spoke I knew she had an Achilles' heel. It was the voice from the gramophone record.

CHAPTER SIX

Marcia Garnett spoke with unhurried confidence in a low, clear voice that was audible in every part of the room, replying, briefly but wittily, to the toast and only at the end touching on the loss to her profession of the late Cyprian Druse, adding the fact that, though her weekly article on the cinema had appeared on the same page of the same paper as his, it was her profound regret that she had never met him in person.

How strange it was, I was thinking, that the women who had known my uncle either fell over backwards to convince me how intimate they had been with him or else they went to unnecessary lengths to establish that they had never set eyes on him.

The grouping at the tables was breaking up; people moving about and joining other tables, hailing their friends and their enemies. I asked Anstey to introduce me to Miss Garnett, but it seemed there were people I had to meet first, and it was, after all, Anstey's party.

D. L. Pritchard, a long-jowled female writer of thrillers, one of our clients who was beginning to sell very well in America, was our first quarry. She was wearing a full-evening dress of two colours of brocade, swathed from either shoulder in the period rather early between the two world wars. Her arms were bare and muscular and rather brown. She wrung my hand with a powerful grip, asked us to sit down and offered me a cigarette, commenting with caustic wit on the horrors of literary gatherings, and literary women in particular. I asked what were the hopes of the completion of the second book on the American contract we had arranged for her and she told me it was more than half done. That is the sort of thing any agent is pleased to hear—if he has his wits about him and is not obsessed with a dusky-voiced blonde—so I relinquished all present thought of the chase and discussed a policy of magazine articles which we might place judiciously to coincide with the book's publication, as well as the remoter possibility of a follow-up lecture tour.

Miss Pritchard was brisk, businesslike and most willing to co-operate, but after a few minutes she said, "Look, you don't want to waste any more time over me, now. Go along and meet all the interesting people and run down and see me when there's nothing going on in town. Stay with me a couple of days if you like and bring a friend. I've got a cottage at Barrow Lock. Anstey'll tell you."

"That's very nice of you," I said.

"Not a bit," she said. "You'll be clay in my hands on my own ground. All this paralyses me. Just give me a ring. So long as you don't mind cats."

I said, "Thanks very much, I'd love to. You're fond of cats?"

"No, come to think of it, I'm not," she answered, "but they adore me. I find them waiting on the doorstep even before I move into a house. The theory is that I'm a witch. Anyway, I've given up the struggle and just let them have the run of any place I happen to occupy. So long as you don't mind."

Anstey bore me away. "Funny thing," he said as we moved out of earshot, "she does quite a lot of verse under the name of Cynthia Spalding. The exact opposite of her murder stories and not a bit of good to us, but of course we have to handle the stuff, now that she's selling so well."

Staggered, I paused in my stride to look over my shoulder and try and connect this rather hearty, intelligent adult with the frighteningly girlish, now harsh, now shrill utterance of the record to which the press cutting of Cyprian's criticism had been clipped. So this was the woman who had dedicated a poem called *Immaculate Despoiler* to my uncle. I found it impossible to imagine her despoilation taking any but an immaculate form.

"Have you stayed at her cottage?" I asked.

"No," said Anstey rather hastily, but not meeting my eyes, "but it would pay you to run down. There's a very decent pub at Barrow Lock that would put you up if you don't like cats. It's called the Sitting Hen."

"Of course," I said. "That's the place Mandrake was talking about."

"You've met Mandrake, have you?" Anstey looked pleasantly surprised.

I explained, without overdoing it.

"Yes, Mandrake used to live near there until he moved to Pimlico earlier this year," Anstey told me. "One of those little colonies of the intelligentsia has been settling there for the past few years; a cross between what Chelsea is supposed to be and what part of Cornwall *is;* has its headquarters at the Sitting Hen. Your uncle ran almost a debating club there on fine week ends."

A retired major, whose armchair reminiscences had astonishingly but successfully been dramatised, now had to be placated, for it seems our firm had previously assured him that there were to his product no dramatic rights worth considering, and he had a tremendous gloat to get off his chest. Our backs were to another group, and now, before I had realised who was in it, I heard Anstey saying, "Miss Garnett, here's a friend of ours from America who would like to meet you. Simon Crane —Marcia Garnett."

I caught my breath as she turned, still half laughing at somebody's joke, and, full of detached sociability, put out a hand to me, not having taken in my name.

"How do you do?" we both demanded, and I knew that much about England to recognise this as a question I didn't have to answer. Instead I said, "I enjoyed your speech."

She offered me the meaningless, complimented smile of a woman who is accustomed to compliments. "American, didn't Mr. Anstey say?" she said. "How long have you been over?"

"Since Friday."

"Then I suppose you came on the *Queen Mary?*"

"I did," I agreed, "but nobody on the dock even asked me what I thought about British pictures."

We laughed and then she said, "But if you were a prize fighter they'd have asked you—and you don't *look* like a music-hall turn . . ."

I said, "Don't we export anything else?"

"Well, if you do, it doesn't get into the papers."

"And of course you only believe what you read in the papers?"

"Well, I suppose one or two human beings get smuggled across once in a way. Do you come into that category?"

"By no means," I assured her, smiling. "I'm a literary agent."

"Now why?" she asked, clearly determined to do right,

conversationally, by her country's guest, and keep things within easy reach of his intelligence. "What makes a man choose that profession of all professions?"

It was one of those questions that provide you with a nice open space in which to make a fool of yourself, and already she was only half listening for the answer. I could shoot off on that to my heart's content, she was thinking, while she kept an expression on her face and got ready to move on to more interesting fields as soon as honour had been satisfied. If any two people in the world had something to say to one another, we had, and yet she was forcing me into a labyrinth of polite conversation that must occupy us until it was too late to say anything.

"A love of literature and a desire to serve humanity," I said shortly, and, I hoped, cynically. "And what prompted you to shed your lustre on criticism of the cinema?"

She must have felt my exasperation, for her smile was suddenly genuine. "A living to earn, a passion for words and not enough imagination to invent stories," she said.

"You could have become an intellectual and dispensed with any story."

"I said I had a living to earn."

"If you had cared a hoot why I became an agent," I said, "the answer would have been almost identical. Except that I write the stories anyway." I don't know what was driving me to these extremes of self-revelation but I added, "And man and boy, I've sold five so far to schoolboys' magazines."

She laughed, but not cruelly, and then said in a half-shocked voice, "Do you know I once had a story read in the children's hour at the B.B.C. It was called 'Humpty and Dumpty Catch the Country Bus.' " She paused for a moment and then said regretfully, "I never meant even to remember that. It's been the skeleton in my cupboard ever since I grew up. I only told you so that you'd feel comfortable about the schoolboys' magazines."

I didn't smile now but met her eyes quite soberly. "What makes you think I shan't expose you?" I asked.

"Surely making fools of people is too easy to be worth while?"

"You ought to know," I answered quietly. "There were moments when I felt quite a fool last night in the Green Bar beyond the swimming pool. . . ."

For a second she was taken off guard and her eyes widened. "Just a moment," she said, "I didn't . . ."

"Quite catch the name?" I helped her. "Crane, Simon Crane."

Anstey had moved straight on to another group and had now returned with a man and woman to whom he evidently wanted to introduce me. I shall never know who they were nor what they looked like, for all the time I was shaking hands automatically I was watching each muscle harden in Marcia's perfectly masking face and her eyes focus sharply as she measured her adversary. Nothing in her look or manner gave any indication of her state of mind, but somewhere in her throat a tiny, rhythmic pulse began to stir the ice-blue ruffle.

"Mr. Anstey was just telling me," the woman was saying. "What a terrible shock for you, arriving at your uncle's flat like that to find him dead."

My tongue worked quicker than my brain. Giving the words no weight of special significance, I turned towards her and said, "It was a shock certainly, but it would be foolish for me to pretend to personal sorrow. Like Miss Garnett, I'm one of the few people here who had never met my uncle."

From the corner of my eye I saw the muscles soften and the tension relax from Marcia Garnett's face, as she realised that if I believed she hadn't met him, I couldn't have played her record. I didn't want her as relaxed as all that, so I put over a fast one. "But it's extraordinary the number of people who still ring him up," I said, "even people who have never met him. It's quite an adventure living in his flat."

"It must be," said Marcia Garnett. "Like an adventure from a schoolboys' magazine."

Oho, I thought, so it's gloves off and no holds barred between us. Anstey had taken my arm again and was trying to steer me in a new direction. I dug my heels into the carpet and said, with a commendably casual air, "If you're really so interested in those first editions of Cyprian's, Miss Garnett, why not drop in for a sherry tomorrow evening?" For she would hardly dare to leave things as they were, and here was an easy way for her to find out what I knew or to convince me of what she wanted me to believe about her dealings with my uncle.

She met my eyes uncertainly, conceding nothing, but she didn't say, "Whoever mentioned first editions?"

"I'm a stranger in a strange land," I went on. "Who knows, perhaps I could persuade you to dine?"

"Perhaps you could," she replied, unsmiling. "Who knows?"

And then Anstey yielded me up to a seedy-looking ex-schoolmaster, the film rights of whose sex-ridden historical novel were being hotly bidden for. I was obliged to engage him in conversation, but all the time I was conscious of her, aware, through the back of my neck, that she was equally conscious of me and perhaps afraid. At last I was able to look over my shoulder and found that she was not there at all. She had gone and her party had gone, leaving flatness unendurable. I tried to get away then, but Anstey was insatiable on my behalf. Not till the last group broke up was I permitted to go.

Out in the cool dark he offered me a lift in his taxi, but I wanted to walk and think and be ready for her next move.

Marcia Garnett; I knew her name. I knew the tilt of her head and the breath of her perfume. I knew her business and the whole polished perfection of her façade. I knew, too, how she spoke to the man she loved and how her eyes looked through the man who could harm her. I knew too much.

And as the cool night air gradually penetrated even to my common sense it occurred to me that, knowing how efficiently Anstey would detain me, she had left the party a good while ahead of me, and for all I knew she was back at my flat rifling it more efficiently the second time. I set about getting a taxi at once, but when I got back to the flat everything was as I had left it. No perfume lingered on the air; no atmosphere of recent human warmth assailed my senses as I let myself in; nothing. I was absurdly disappointed, and then I thought, but of course she has no purpose in coming by stealth now that I know who she is and have asked her to come. She will come tomorrow by invitation. I went to bed tired out and ridiculously happy.

I was awake before dawn, like a boy anticipating his first tryst. It seemed altogether wrong that I should take so light a heart with me to my uncle's funeral. To my surprise, Mandrake was there before me though there seemed to be no relations taking any interest. Our branch of the family had long ago lost all contacts in this country, but I presumed the solicitor would have informed anyone who ought to know. A telegram had arrived from the Orkneys saying, "Please spend ten shillings on wreath for me. P.O. follows. Hannah Druse." I had carried out this commission and added another wreath for my mother and one for myself, and I watched them lower the last of Cyprian into the earth.

Stripped of its verbiage, my uncle's will stated that he was aware that he had lived beyond his income, but that in the event of there being anything over, it was to go to my mother. His personal effects were to be mine except for the gramophone records, which went to his musical colleague on the *Reviewer,* his first editions, which went to his club, and his portraits and busts—all of himself—which were each left to a specified West End theatre.

Mandrake, who was heartbroken to have been unable to get to the inquest, waited for me so that I could tell him the gist of the will, but he could find no motive for murder in it. He asked me to lunch, but I was already late for an appointment and had to hurry away. I had to lunch with the reminiscing major and then to look in at the office and let Anstey know the result. Anstey gave me an indifferent tea and asked me to go with him to a first night, but I got out of it and managed to leave him in time to get to a florist before it closed. As I entered Pendervil Mansions it occurred to me that, apart from my uncle's excellent sherry, I had nothing whatever to offer a guest and I turned down the alley of shops to the pastry cook's at the end. They were putting up the shutters and were neither pleased to see me nor interested in my suggestion that they should find me some little cakes or biscuits or petits fours. They had nothing, nothing at all, and they didn't look sorry. There was a girl inside, just paying for an unwrapped brown loaf which she held in her hand. She followed me out as I left.

"Too bad," she said. "I've just bought their last loaf of Hovis, if half of that would be any use."

I looked closely. It was Mrs. Best's sister Hazel, whose other name I didn't know.

I said, "Thanks very much, but I don't think it would. It was something more . . ."

"Special?" she suggested. "It's hopeless at this time. They never have anything edible after midday."

"It doesn't matter," I said, and we began to cross the courtyard to our block of the flats. After a moment's deliberation she said, "If it's really important, I *have* got half a pound of chocolate biscuits."

"Well, that would do better than nothing," I said, totally unaware that the offer of half a pound of chocolate biscuits in England, now, practically amounted to a declaration of love. My problem solved, I asked her, for no good reason, if she read the *New Statesman*.

"Well, only passively."

"I understood that one read it actively or not at all."

"You've been misinformed. There are a number of border-line cases; people who only read it when they happen on a copy, and *they* mostly read it backwards."

"How do you mean?"

"Starting with the advertisements, which couldn't happen anywhere else, we move steadily back through the competitions, taking in a little film or dramatic criticism on the way to This England, after which we might just read the Sagittarius poem before taking our stand on the last paragraph of the London Diary, which quite often contains a joke."

We had reached the door of her flat, which I stayed churlishly outside for fear of meeting Myrtle Best, while Hazel

74

fetched the biscuits, and then even more churlishly I offered to pay for them, but, "Oh no," said Hazel firmly. "*Money* doesn't buy chocolate biscuits. You take them as a gift or not at all." So I took them as a gift.

Back in my own flat I found three of Cyprian's Cretan jugs and arranged my flowers in them: dark red peonies on the dark polished wood of three little tables, while my mind ran forward over the words of the conversation that I should have with Marcia Garnett. I engineered it so that she had to make all the running, planning the moves to force her to commit herself every time. For I held the trump card and she knew it and couldn't afford to leave it in my hands. She would have to come and she shouldn't go till I was satisfied with her story.

I began to worry about what sort of combination the sherry would make with the chocolate biscuits, and at last, leaving the sherry with the glasses on the tray on the desk, moved the biscuits to the top of a low bookcase, where I could ignore them, or happen upon them casually, as though I hadn't really known they were there. "Oh, chocolate biscuits," I could say. "Good old Brady," or, if they clearly weren't what Marcia Garnett could care about, "Brady really is a fool at times." As I planned each move in the encounter I was placing chairs at strategic points so that the light must fall on her face, rearranging cushions, adding casual touches, while I smoked innumerable cigarettes, and one by one the petals of the full-blown peonies, which had been upheld by the stiff white florist's paper, came loose from their stems and dropped with sudden startling taps onto the polished Queen Anne tables.

By eight o'clock I knew she wasn't coming. By half-past eight I had dialled Directory Enquiries and the G.P.O. and the police and even the offices of the *Sunday Reviewer,* but not one of them could, or, at all events, would, tell me the home address of Marcia Garnett. At nine Mandrake came.

He had in his hands, besides a notebook and pencil, a bound volume of crossword puzzles, a couple of comic papers and a foreign copy of *Vogue,* marked seven and sixpence. He looked glowingly happy and seemed delighted to find me in.

"Wonderful," he said. "I called this afternoon, but you weren't here. I thought I'd go away and do a little research and come back."

He sat down and I poured him a sherry. There was no need to offer him a chocolate biscuit, for those he had found already.

"What did you mean by research?" I asked.

"That was only to fill the time till I found you," said Mandrake. "I've been terribly handicapped, not being able to get hold of you and know how things are progressing. Now what did you make of that little actress turning out to have given us a false name and being newly engaged to Paul Cleveland? It gave her a stronger motive, but I can't believe she killed him."

"Nor can I, although it was suspicious that she should happen to ring up Cyprian that night of all nights."

"I think it was quite natural," said Mandrake after a moment. "She'd just got engaged, and so she had suddenly more to lose than ever before. She telephoned, meaning to persuade Druse to give her back the record. Instead she spoke to you, who seemed willing to help her. I don't believe she knew he was dead before we told her. Do you?"

"Not on the surface, no, but we have to remember she's an actress. That might make a difference."

"Not a great deal, from what I know of women," said Mandrake, "though heaven knows that isn't much. I'm entering her as having sufficient motive, for the present. Now don't you think we ought to play the other records?"

"They aren't here any more." I felt guilty and awkward in the extreme.

Mandrake swung upon me. "What happened?"

"I gave one up to the brother of the woman who made it. She was newly married and when she read that the collection was to be sold she'd threatened to kill herself. Her brother was demented. I went to the house and met her. She couldn't have killed Cyprian. She had an alibi. She was on her honeymoon."

"Was her brother on his honeymoon?" said Mandrake.

"I didn't think of that."

"Never mind. It's done now. Let's enter what you know."

I told him the name and address of Mrs. Creel, who made the "suicide" record, and the name of her brother, whom he added to the suspects, then he leaned back and waited for me to tell him what had happened to the others.

"The rest were stolen," I said, overstating the matter by exactly one record, "on Sunday evening while I was out."

"Were there any clues?"

"No."

"How did they get in?"

"Through the skylight in the kitchen."

"How do you suppose they knew that you were out?"

I didn't tell him the answer to that one. I didn't want him to be talking to me at all, worming nearer and nearer to the fact that I was pretty certain in my own mind who *had* done the murder, and that she had outwitted me once more and that I was aching to be back at the telephone trying to wrest her address by some means from someone.

With infinite precision, Mandrake had added the information I had given him to his chart, then he said, "I decided to follow up the *New Statesman* clue when you weren't in. I went to the three nearest news agents in the district and got them to let me see their delivery lists. It took a bit of doing. I had to buy something from each of them before I could gain their confidence; that's why I got back so late."

"But don't they close about half-past five?"

"I don't make myself clear. One of my purchases was this volume of puzzles. I had never essayed one before. After I left the news agents I rang your flat and, getting no answer, I walked to the Embankment, sat on a seat and opened the volume. I became deeply involved and only realised the time some ten minutes ago. But here"—he happily spread out a folded sheet of foolscap—"I have a list of every regular subscriber to the *New Statesman* in the district."

"What makes you suppose the murderer resides in the district?"

"I don't, but he's got to live somewhere and we know that he reads the *New Statesman*."

Trying not to let my lack of enthusiasm communicate itself to him, I took the sheet and my eyes wandered down the list. The name on the fourth line leapt out from the paper and engaged my eye as surely as though it had been in a different colour from the rest. Marcia Garnett was a regular reader of the *New Statesman* and she lived at Flat 609, Pendervil Mansions, on the same floor, three flats away from me.

CHAPTER SEVEN

Mandrake was leaning forward with his eyes alight. "There's someone there," he said, "isn't there? A name you recognise? Someone you suspect?"

"No, nothing like that," I said hastily, but I might as well have tried to stem Vesuvius as conceal my darling from his remorseless pursuit. "But your face is entirely different. You were bored when I came. You were trying to get rid of me. Now you're excited. You're even breathing faster. One of these names belongs to someone you suspect."

There was only one thing I could think of that would account for what he saw without doing any worse. "Not someone I suspect at all," I said. "It's the name of the woman I fell in love with last night at the Critics' Group dinner."

Mandrake's whole opinion of human nature took a fearful jolt. "You tell me you could fall in love at a time like this—and at a place like that?" he moaned. "How can I hope to get any co-operation whatsoever?"

"You can't," I said. "I'm as sorry about it as you are. It's the last thing I meant to do."

Mandrake's face grew thoughtful, almost sympathetic. "She was irresistible?" he enquired very quietly.

I nodded.

"Are you quite sure that it wasn't a blind?"

So here he was, back again, stumbling flat-footed onto the right trail, for the wrong reason. "Supposing she too wanted something out of you, or something out of your uncle's flat, supposing she were clever or had more to lose than her sisters, mightn't she prove irresistible if she met you at a Critics' Group dinner?"

"There'd have to be rather a lot of coincidence involved."

"There's a printed list of the guests at that dinner. She could have seen it in advance and played up to you deliberately."

I remembered how she had looked when she realised my name. "I'm perfectly certain she didn't know I'd be there."

"Then she knew who you were? She'd have known your name if she saw it?"

He would have the facts out of me yet, if I didn't think quicker than he could. I said, "She'd never seen me before and I'd never seen her; and she didn't play up in the least. I think she found me rather dull. I fell in love all by myself."

"And she didn't know your name?"

"Not unless she'd happened to see it in that paragraph in the *Recorder*."

"Which, incidentally, you have never explained to me. How could they know that your uncle had left you his records?"

"He didn't," I told him. "I thought if that paragraph were published the people who'd made them might get in touch with me to try and get them back."

Mandrake looked crestfallen. "And you never told *me*," he said. "While I tell you *everything*." Very softly, so as not to lose this slight advantage, he added, "Since you do not suspect her, it can do no harm for me to know the name of the lady you so admire." He looked down his foolscap list, saying the names as he went. When he came to Marcia he raised his head

79

and smiled. "Marcia Garnett writes criticism which they say almost raises the cinema to the status of an art. Who would be likelier than she, out of this list, to grace the Critics' Group dinner?"

I could have cut his throat, but he was rapt with happiness at his own deductive skill and gathering momentum every minute. "And I see that she lives under the same roof, on the same floor, in fact. And yet did you tell me that it was at *first sight* that you fell in love with her at the dinner? That you'd never seen her face or heard her voice before?"

I hadn't told him that but I instantly did.

"Very well then." His face hardened. I felt that he had decided it was no use seeking my co-operation and he must get his information by stealth. "Let us waste no more time on her but concentrate our attention on the people whose voices you *did* hear. Since the records are no longer available and I, alas, never heard them, we'd better lose no time in noting down all the details you remember, while they're still fairly fresh in your memory."

"Certainly," I said, glad to take the conversation away from Marcia. "You've noted Mrs. Creel already, she's just a frail, foolish little woman with an alibi; Janet Drury, the actress, you've met yourself and can draw your own conclusions. Then there was a record from Myrtle Best, a pseudo-intellectual widow who has the flat below this. It was she who noticed blood dripping on her window sill. She claims a deep and beautiful relationship with Cyprian, but he'd written 'The Sacred Cow' on the label of her record, so I fancy it may have been one-sided. She's a blonde and says she was in the fish queue at the time of the murder."

Mandrake wrote busily. "And then?"

"There was the one marked 'Lisle Street,' that had plainly been made by a street walker. Just a piece of showing-off on Cyprian's part, I fancy, with no indication who she was. I think we can dismiss her. Then there was a painfully embarrassing one from a poetess called Cynthia Spalding. She'd sent him a published volume of love poetry along with the record which was sort of a dedication to him, I gathered. He seemed to have published a witheringly cruel review of the verses and the cutting was clipped to the record."

"Is the volume in his bookshelves?"

"Yes. Would you like me to find it?"

"Of course."

I got up and began to comb my uncle's library. I had no recollection at all where I had replaced the book. I had been talking quickly but Mandrake's notes had kept pace with me. "Go on. That's five."

I saw the trap he had laid for me and stepped over it. "That's the lot," I said, beginning to search a new bookshelf.

"That's only five," persisted Mandrake. "You told me six."

"No, definitely five." My heart began to creak, for I am a poor liar and Mandrake was a most difficult person to lie to.

"Did you? Ah well, perhaps I was wrong." He pondered his list. "But there was one you spoke of the other evening, the last you'd played, you said, made by someone who had known him better than the others, and who revealed much more about him."

"That must have been Myrtle Best," I said rather wildly. "I told you she claimed a deep and beautiful friendship with him."

"I see," said Mandrake, then, "No, I don't. If her claim were genuine, he wouldn't have called her 'The Sacred Cow,' now would he?"

"Possibly not," I agreed, racking my brains for some escape from his remorseless intrusiveness. "Well, Mrs. Best only lives downstairs. I'll introduce you. She'll talk on the slightest provocation. As a matter of fact, I have to go out myself, but we could drop in on the way."

"No, thank you. Another time, perhaps, but not tonight. I feel so certain that if you really concentrate you'll be able to remember more than you've told me, but the longer we put it off the less chance there'll be of your remembering accurately. You see, we've only your memory to go on, and everyone's memory is faulty."

"But of course. I'm not claiming to be infallible."

"And after all, you only heard them once."

"All but one," I thought while I agreed with him.

"Isn't it possible that the excitement of your uncle's death and the—considerable emotional upheaval of falling in love—might have caused you to—overlook one record?"

"Perfectly possible," I agreed, for by now I had realised that I'd been a fool to pretend there'd been only five. I should have done much better to *invent* a sixth voice and personality and let him enter *those* particulars on his list than try to fob him off with only five.

"Because, you see, I can't get away from the conviction that you spoke of a much more interesting voice than you've described tonight. I am certain you mentioned one woman who was no fool." He watched me narrowly. "Doesn't that call up anything to mind? It certainly doesn't apply to any of the five I have entered here. Just think a minute."

A few more minutes under that hypnotic gaze and I might have told him anything, but fortune permitted me to find the volume of Miss Spalding's verse, and I laid it on the desk before him. That at least might take his mind off the moment.

"Thanks," he said, putting it in his pocket. "I'll look into that when I get home. Meantime, don't you think we really ought to go over the flat with a fine-tooth comb for clues to the burglary? After all, if we'd handed this thing over to the police they'd do that automatically. If we're to justify ourselves for keeping it in our own hands, I don't think we ought to leave any stone unturned."

"Nor the back of the kitchen cabinet, either, for all I know," I thought desperately. Something of the panic in my brain would communicate itself to him, and he would find it and be playing Marcia's record itself while I hovered and did nothing. I decided to get myself and the record out of the flat, where we could do no more harm, and then he could search for clues to his heart's content.

"I suppose it should be done," I agreed, "only, as I told you, I have to go out."

"I'll come with you."

"Oh, don't feel you have to do that. You're perfectly welcome to stay and search the flat. There are bound to be fingerprints."

"I'm not equipped to deal with fingerprints," said Mandrake coldly, for I knew this as well as he did; besides, he wanted to know where I was going. "I'll come too. I could do with a walk."

"Thanks, but I'd rather be alone."

"That's all right. I won't talk."

"No, really. I prefer my own society at times."

"All right. But I've got to be moving myself. I'll just see you on your way, and go on my own way home."

His was the trusting charm of a child and I betrayed his trust. "Very well," I said briskly, "come along." I walked into the kitchen, selected a thin-bladed knife from the drawer, then, untying the rope, I withdrew the flat parcel from behind the cabinet, scaled the few rungs of the fire escape and had pushed open the skylight. I paused, just long enough to see him, sitting defeated on the sink, and there I left him, for even the heart of a child couldn't have coaxed Mandrake's vast bulk through the skylight and onto the roof.

I had to climb three little walls and cross two roof gardens to get to the roof which I calculated must be hers. The skylight was only a crack open, but the thin line of light told me there was someone in the flat. I inserted the long blade and moved it till it encountered the rope, then I sawed gently till I felt it give and the window swung upward and open at a tug from my fingers. The metal stairs were below, running down into the kitchen as they did in my own flat. I crouched, to see the kitchen was empty, then swung my feet over the ledge and began to descend, rung by rung.

She might throw me out, certainly, but I should be in first, and I had my opening lines ready. Just for this once, fortune was on my side. Miss Garnett was being molested. I heard voices as soon as I'd got my head below roof level, hers and a soft, persuasive, faintly Celtic voice that might have had just half a drink too many. The kitchen door was ajar and somewhere just beyond it in the adjoining room the owner of the Celtic voice was trying to kiss her, but he was not trying very hard as yet.

"Go away," I heard her say, wearily, not even angrily. "Oh, Uncle Stephen, please go away."

"I'll go," said the other voice, "in my own good time. I've only just found you. I'm parched for the sight of you and the feel of you in my arms."

"You never had me in your arms," her voice blazed into anger, "and you never will. Oh, please, why don't you think of Aunt Mabel?"

"That's what you said all along," the voice came thicker. "That's how you've fobbed me off over and over, as if she need have known. That's why you ran away from us both and that's why I've followed you. And we don't have to think of Mabel any more. She isn't here."

"I'm afraid you've misunderstood me. I only asked *you* to think of Mabel because she's a hundred times too good for you anyway. But it isn't the thought of her that makes me resist you; that's pure self-interest."

"In other words, I'm repulsive to you?" The voice was growing truculent.

"In any language."

"You didn't always find me so detestable."

"That's not true. There were times when she was in the room and I couldn't show it. If I'd moved away every time you sat too close to me or paid me a compliment, it would have brought it even more plainly to her attention."

"So you tolerated me to avoid upsetting my wife?"

"If you want to hear me say so."

"Then here's something more you can tolerate. I've been dreaming of it for months . . ."

"Uncle Stephen . . . please . . ."

There was panic in her voice. I put my parcel on the draining board, pushed open the kitchen door, picked him off her by the scruff of his neck and the seat of his pants and

84

dumped him in the passage. Then I closed the door and leaned my back against it while I straightened my tie. She was standing in front of me, trying to climb back into her composure, but there was bright colour now under her translucent skin and sparks of fire in the blue of her eyes, and from one ruffled strand of her spun-glass hair swung a single silver pin which her fingers found and wove automatically back into her hair. I grinned and said, "Do you mind if I sit down?"

"Mind?" She wrapped herself back inside her armour. "I didn't think my preference would have any weight. Had you been standing all that while in the kitchen because no one thought to ask you to sit down?"

"I haven't been there very long. Most of the time I was coming down the ladder."

"So you got in from the roof? Is that your usual method of visiting?"

"I assure you, no. But I'm a stranger here. And when in Rome one studies the customs of the natives." I bowed in her direction so that she could not fail to grasp that I knew she had burgled my flat by the same method.

She moved across the room with me following and sat on the settee while I took a facing chair and offered her a cigarette, which she refused without telling me to light up. She was giving nothing. If it happened that I was in her flat and at ease in it, I had got there under my own power for what good it did me. The fact that I happened to have done her some small service in getting rid of her drunken admirer was purely coincidental and wasn't going to help me. It was each for himself.

"You wanted to see me?"

If we were playing it that way, I had some cards too. "Yes," I said, "it's about my uncle's murder." And I watched the colour drain away from her face so that the cheekbones stood out sharply, and, oddly enough, she looked younger than before.

Her eyes grew large and she never said a word, only reached for a cigarette from the box that stood near on the table. I was quicker and had offered my case a second time, so that she took one without thinking, and I had lit it before she realised how she had weakened her position and, pushing the box, said, "Won't you?"

Consolidating my advantage, I said, "No, thanks, I never touch them," and put my lighter away and leaned back to let her break the silence when she chose. Presently she said:

"You think Cyprian was murdered?"

"I know."

Her eyebrows shot up. "And the police?"

"Don't know."

"Oho." The corners of her mouth twinkled. "You're in this on your own, then? Cowboys and Indians?" You couldn't hold the advantage over a woman like that for long.

"You're behind the times," I said, "but you've got the idea."

She stubbed out the unsmoked cigarette and clasped her hands round her knees. "Who murdered him?" she said.

"Suppose you tell *me?*"

For a moment her eyes looked straight and startled into mine. Then she dropped her lashes. "Yes, this is a slight advance on the cowboy technique, but that's not the way we're going to play it. For one thing, I've not the slightest idea who did it, if it was done. How do you know he was murdered, and why was he and by whom?"

"It was done by a woman," I said. "A woman who was at one time in love with him, and had either grown out of it or was afraid she'd give in to him and lose her individuality; or she had fallen in love with someone else and was afraid Cyprian might harm her."

"Very feasible, but mightn't it equally be an actress that he'd slated or a poet that he'd damned with faint praise or a novelist he'd parodied or a playwright he'd ridiculed? Aren't you narrowing the field too much?"

"Only to six."

"Six?"

"Six voices, trapped on wax, locked in a cabinet; six women whom he'd persuaded to make fools of themselves in special

86

ways to cheat time of its disillusionment for him, when he ceased to fascinate; six creatures who, once he'd tired of them, once they knew it, would never lie quiet an hour in their beds while they believed those records to exist. Out of the six, one and one only had the strength of character and the determination to gamble Cyprian's life against her peace of mind, and Cyprian lost his life. Only she didn't get her record back, and whether she won her peace of mind or not is hard to say, isn't it?"

"Hard to say?" she repeated, sharply and superciliously. "Don't tell me *you* find difficulty in expressing yourself about *anything?*"

Oddly enough the small barb heartened me. If she thought I was an easy talker, that meant she couldn't hear my heart thumping and there was hope I might complete the interview without mentioning that if there was any little thing she wanted fetched, like the moon or the Milky Way, to count me in.

I said, "You asked me what I knew about my uncle's murder. If I'm boring you I can stop." And I stopped.

After a moment she leaned forward. "Why are you so certain it was murder? I read how the body was found. How could it be anything but accident?"

"Because Cyprian wasn't alone that afternoon. There was someone heard in his flat at almost the exact time of his death."

"The papers said he was alone all the afternoon."

"They didn't know."

"Was there anything to prove someone had been there?"

"There was a piece torn out of the *New Statesman* between the body and the window sill."

"Well, that's not conclusive. It could have come from Cyprian's own copy."

"For a person who never met him you know a lot about my uncle. No, someone had removed the torn copy after he was dead and taken it away. And they must have brought it with them in the first place. Cyprian's copy was intact on the desk."

"So the murderer was a reader of the *New Statesman*."

"Yes. I gather that indicates a special type?"

"Quite a number of special types. But I wouldn't call it primarily a woman's paper. Why are you determined that your uncle's visitor was a woman?"

I put the wing-shaped crystal earring into her hand and explained how I found it. "Anyone might have shed an earring at any time," she reasoned. "It needn't be connected with his death."

"Not necessarily, but I think this was." I handed her the fragment of silvery hairpin. "It was used in an attempt to pick the lock of the record cabinet," I explained.

"A bit of wire?" she asked, her fingers curling over it.

"A broken hairpin. What sort of woman do you suppose would use a hairpin of that colour?"

She smiled levelly. "A woman with my colour hair, a woman with snow-white hair, a pessimist with greying hair or a slut with any colour hair."

"Then it was one out of that selection who also possessed an undisciplined heart and a disciplined brain."

"Why?"

"A disciplined heart wouldn't have become involved with my uncle Cyprian, and I take it an undisciplined brain would have no dalliance with the *New Statesman*."

"But only a disciplined murderer would provide himself with reading matter in case he ran into unforeseen delay."

"I don't think the killing was premeditated. I think the murderer went there for some other purpose and that when, for some reason, Cyprian leaned out of the window, she saw her chance and took it. I feel sure it could only have happened like that."

"You sound as though that's important to you."

"It is."

"Why?"

She had risen and was moving towards the window, seeming not even to be very interested in the answer to her question.

For no reason at all that I shall ever understand, I answered with the bare, fantastic truth. "I've fallen in love with her."

As she stood, caught in her stride, looking at me over her shoulder, colour slowly crept up and flooded her face. But for that, she might still have pretended that she didn't think I was speaking about her. But now we were both in the open.

CHAPTER EIGHT

She said, "You're certain I killed him?"

"No one else had so much character," I answered. "No one else had so much to lose."

Her face was bitter. Only one thing could have told me anything about her character. "I suppose you *had* to play the records?"

"What would you have done? Someone had tried to pick the lock of the record cabinet that afternoon. It seemed that the reason for his death must be inside."

She was slowly pacing the room. "And you think it was?"

"Yes."

"Then why are you here? Why didn't you go to the police?"

"You know the answer to that."

"You fell in love?"

I didn't answer.

"Then what *were* you going to do?" She didn't sound at all deeply concerned, merely curious in a detached, half-amused way. I felt limp and absurd.

"I don't know," I admitted foolishly. "I wanted to see you; to try and understand you. I suppose in my heart I hoped we could become friends."

She gave a short laugh. "You surely must see that any sort of friendship is out of the question between us. Would any woman willingly remain in any room where there's a man who's heard her expose and humiliate herself as I did when I made that damnable record? Don't you think I wake in the night, sweating, when I realise it exists? But I knew he'd never play it to anyone, and whether I'd known it or not, I'd probably have made it, then. I don't know what it was that he had, but he had it and he could do what he wanted with most of us. . . . Almost what he wanted—not quite, as it happens in my case, but I don't expect you to believe that."

I said, "I want to believe everything you tell me. But it doesn't make any difference."

"You don't care whether I'm honest or a liar?"

"Oh yes, I care. But it doesn't alter the way I feel. You don't care about people for reasons. You get fond of them and then try to find excuses to justify yourself. If you can't find any excuses it's just too bad, but you go on caring anyway, sometimes worse, and sometimes hating yourself for operating without any relationship to your brain."

She said, "You have the situation between me and Cyprian in a nutshell."

"You and me and Cyprian," I said, "we seem to have been a vicious circle."

"Only Cyprian wasn't in love with you. I'd call it more of a cul-de-sac." She smiled, the saddest, emptiest smile. "Cyprian's dead and I'm glad he's dead, and you're alive, so far. You think I killed him to try and get back that record. Aren't you afraid that I might kill you?"

"Not really," I said. "Not afraid."

"I suppose, with your technicolour attitude to life, you were looking forward to it?"

The telephone rang. She took the receiver. "Hullo?" she said, and then her voice warmed and softened into ordinary kindliness that I'd never heard in it before. "Mabel," she said, "darling, it's ages since I've spoken to you . . . if I didn't sometimes hear it on the radio I'd forget the sound of your voice. . . . I know, but I've been so terribly busy, I couldn't have got away. . . . Darling, yes, the country must be looking wonderful but . . . Oh"—her voice changed entirely—"then you're on your own? . . . Edinburgh? But, darling, are you *sure* he's *gone?* . . . No, nothing, only Uncle Stephen isn't usually very reliable, is he? . . . Oh well, if you bought him the ticket there isn't much else he could be up to, is there? You know, I don't believe there's a thing I can't get out of on my diary for the next couple of days. Shall I just check up in the morning and let you know? All right. Good-bye, darling. Don't work too hard."

She replaced the receiver, smiling, and turned to me with a businesslike air. "And now, young man," she said briskly, "I've no more time to waste. I'm afraid you're going to be let down rather badly, and in such an odd way. You're incredibly young and you've built up a front for me; a false, fantastic front. You're a shipwrecked mariner, aren't you, broken by the tides of passion at the foot of the rocks on which I'm combing my bright hair and luring you on with my deadly fascinations? And the rocks are strewn with the bones of the fools that came before. But it's all false. I didn't kill anyone; there were never any fools. I'm neither damned nor deadly nor fascinating. And I've got an aunt Mabel."

She smiled at me almost apologetically.

"But," I said, resenting the illogicality of her reasoning, which had, nonetheless, convinced me, "whether you've got an aunt Mabel or not, somebody killed Cyprian."

"That may be," she answered. "And if it should turn out *not* to be me, what will you do, transfer your adoration to the next suspect or hand her over to the police?"

I said, "You've stolen the evidence against everyone else."

"Evidence?"

"The other records. They were in the cabinet when you telephoned me to meet you in the bar. They were gone when I got back."

"That doesn't prove I took them."

"No, but I believe you did."

"You believe I murdered him."

"Now that I've talked to you, I'm not sure, in spite of the evidence. But I'd be far more inclined to take your word if you told me the truth about the records."

"I've told you the truth all along. Yes, I took the records."

"Why?"

"Because I wanted my own destroyed so badly. When I found I'd gone to all that trouble for nothing, and I realised that those other four records in my hands were as humiliating to four other women as mine was to me, it seemed rather a sanitary gesture to get rid of them. I didn't realise I was destroying four motives for murder and leaving my own sticking out a mile, or I might not have been so public-spirited. Or I might."

"If I gave you yours, you'd all start square."

"Are you going to?"

"If you ask for it."

"How high a price do you imagine I place on it?"

I said, "I kept that record because it was the one thing I had that you wanted. I hoped you'd come and get it, but you were prouder than I supposed. But I never intended to try and barter it for anything you might possess."

"What did you intend?"

"I wanted to take you out to dinner, or to lunch or a theatre or ice hockey or the Zoo; whatever people do in England while they're getting to know one another. But you don't have to do that to get your record back. It's on the draining board in your kitchen. After I'd gone you would have found it, and after you'd found it I still hoped you'd come. I hope so still. I shall come back tomorrow at lunch time to ask you."

She took five steps into the kitchen and lifted the parcel from the draining board. Her knuckles whitened as she gripped it and bent the record through the thick paper till it snapped and snapped and snapped again. Then she leaned against the doorway without seeming to realise I was there. I knew she was going to cry and, knowing that here was one woman in the world who wouldn't want to do that on anyone's shoulder, I stepped smartly out of the flat and shut the door.

I almost expected to find Mandrake still sitting on the sink, but he had gone, leaving a short but unresentful note: "I'll ring tomorrow. M."

Next day was Thursday and I had to go to the office in the morning. Anstey asked me to lunch with him but I said I was promised already. I decided not to telephone Marcia. She knew very well I was coming, and to telephone would give her a chance to put me off. I hurried back to Pendervil Mansions to find her flat empty, with a note on the door for parcels to be left with the porter. The porter told me she had left London for a few days but that he could not give me her address. I wandered aimlessly across the courtyard and through the shopping arcade to the main entrance. London had become a waste and a desolation.

As I turned into the main road, somebody spoke my name.

"Simon Crane."

"Hazel."

"You see, you didn't know me."

"I'm sorry. I was thinking."

"People always are."

"Come and have lunch with me."

"I could."

"Lovely. We'd better eat here, hadn't we?"

Her face fell for a second. "Unless there was somewhere where we could see the sunshine. It seems a pity . . ."

For her it was adventure, for me it was a dead loss anyway, since Marcia was gone. "Would we get in anywhere else, at this time?"

"I suppose not. We'd best stay here."

We made our way to the vast, pretentious, artificially lit Pendervil Grill. For I didn't want to think of the sun that was shining, doubtless on Marcia, with her mind calm in the knowledge that her record was destroyed. She had known I was coming but had gone without a thought of me, not even a thought of gratitude that I had restored her record and not waited to see her humble herself with tears. She might have just rung up to say she was going or pencilled me a note. It would have cost her nothing, and the smallest gesture would have lifted me from this bleak misery to the arch of heaven.

And now here I was with this sober child on my hands. I had asked her what shows she had been to and how she was enjoying her visit and she had replied politely but warily until at last she laid down her knife and fork and said, "But you're making conversation."

Feeling rather affronted, I said, "I'm sorry if I'm a bore."

"But you're *not* a bore, are you?" she said gently.

I felt caught out and absurdly guilty, but she tried to reassure me. "Look here, if you're worried or have something you must think about, that's quite all right. It's nice just having lunch, and *I* can think *too*."

She smiled then and got on with her dinner so cheerfully that I found myself looking at her downbent head with something like respect. "You see," she said, "at home I'm secretary to the local Catchment Board and I have lunch every day in the same café. On Monday it's individual meat pies warmed up with gravy and reconstituted potatoes. On Tuesday it's sausages, and Wednesday, sausage-meat fritters. So just eating a meal like this is enough of an adventure."

"And you don't want your mind taken off unless it's something really important?"

"You don't have to be sarcastic. I was just trying to make you feel nice in case you'd rather not talk."

A waitress advanced with a menu. "There's strawberry mousse to follow, or steamed sponge, fruit tart, fruit compote or *gâteau*."

"What's the mousse like?"

"I had it on Tuesday," said Hazel, with a totally noncommittal face which was belied by the fact that she was treading on my foot under the table.

"Very nice," said the waitress.

"I'll have fruit tart," said Hazel.

"So will I," I said firmly.

"There's additional ice cream if you care for it," said the waitress.

"Additional means you have to pay extra for it," said Hazel, and I thought I detected wistfulness in her eyes.

"We'll have two double portions," I said, and the waitress departed.

"The mousse was very pink and tasted of scent."

I said, "Thanks, I gathered that. Is the ice cream all right?"

"It's heaven."

From pitying her I was suddenly envying anyone so young that she could look forward to a double portion of heaven and be sure of getting it, on a plate with pie as well. As for me, I didn't even know where my heaven was, except that she had pretty obviously gone to that Aunt Mabel who had made the telephone call. I tried to remember any of that conversation that would give me some idea where Mabel might be. Marcia had said, "If I never listened to the radio, I'd forget the sound of your voice." Surely that told me something. Mabel . . . could it possibly be the Mabel Grey of the National Quiz? If so, hadn't Mandrake told me she lived at Barrow Lock—and hadn't I a client there and consequently a perfectly good reason for visiting Barrow Lock? But how could I find out if Marcia's aunt *was* Mabel Grey?

Who could tell me? There was only one person I could think of who was likely to do so willingly, and he mightn't even know who was Marcia's aunt. Then I thought, "He will know who is Mabel Grey's husband."

I said, "Hazel, I've just remembered a call I had to make. Can you hold the fort?"

She smiled and let me go. She was only part way through the first ice and there was all the second as well as the pie to salve my conscience. I found a telephone and called up Mandrake.

"Hullo," he said. "I've just rung your flat. Where are you?"

"It doesn't matter. Has Mabel Grey of the National Quiz got a little Celtic husband called Stephen?"

"She has," said Mandrake. "Why?"

"Does he get tight and make passses at pretty women?"

"I should think so."

"They have a house at Barrow Lock, didn't you say?"

"Yes."

"What was the name of the pub near there that you told me about?"

"The Sitting Hen. Why, are you going down there?"

"I've got to see a woman about a lecture tour."

"Mabel?"

"Good lord, no. One of our authors. D. L. Pritchard. She writes thrillers."

"But, Simon, you've got no sense of responsibility. You can't go dashing off to Barrow Lock while we've got this murder on our hands. We haven't even gone over all our suspects yet and checked their alibis. I was going to come over to you this evening and get down to it in earnest."

To excuse myself I said, "D. L. Pritchard is one of them. She writes poetry as Cynthia Spalding and she sent him one of the records that was stolen." Though I did not for one moment imagine that she'd had any hand in the murder.

"Oh. Well, that's different. Look here, you'll never get a room at the Sitting Hen in the middle of August. You might, though, if I rang up and booked, myself. They know me . . ."

"That's awfully good of you," I said gratefully. "Can you spare the time?"

"Oh, I think so. Yes, yes, I think I can get away. Nobody should try to work in weather like this."

"But I never meant——"

"That's all right. I'll probably notice something that might escape you. I'll phone for rooms and come round and pick you up at the flat, shall I? Be round about four-thirty."

He had rung off without waiting for an answer. As I replaced the receiver I began to laugh. Mandrake or no Mandrake, the world had changed colour since I left the grillroom. The wilderness of emptiness that was London was nothing to me any more. I was on my way—almost on my way—to see Marcia—or at least if I didn't see her, I should be near her, know where she was; and surely while I had my mother wit I should find some way of meeting her in the next twenty-four hours.

Hazel watched me come across the restaurant. Her plate was empty but mine was awash with wilted ice cream. I was amazed at her charm and kindliness, her masterly patience and tact. I paid the bill and took her arm. "What can we do till half-past four?" I said.

She looked at me a moment and seemed to catch my happiness and began to laugh. "We could go for a ride on the top of a bus," she said, "or feed the gulls on the Embankment if we'd anything to feed them with, or just walk about in the sun—or I suppose we could go to a tea dance or a movie, if you wanted to do something definite."

There was the look in her eyes that had been there when she explained about the ice cream, and I knew she was afraid I should plump for the regulation entertainment.

"What do we feed gulls on?"

"Bread. It's against the law, but I'm willing to do it if you are."

We bought a loaf at the pastry cook's. The florist was next door. I bought an orchid and pinned it on her primrose linen jacket. "It would look silly on me," she said, but it didn't.

We fed the birds and we rode on buses and walked along the Embankment. Neither of us knew a thing about London. We got lost and found ourselves and were as gay as a couple of truant school children. As we got back to the mansions she said, suddenly serious, "Good-bye. You've given me a lovely time. I hope you have a lovely time with her."

"Who?"

"She let you down. So you took me out to lunch and were miserable. Then you rang her up and she said you could see her at half-past four and you were so happy that you wanted everyone to be happy—and everyone was."

"You've got it all wrong."

"You even bought her a flower and gave it to me."

"I bought it for you."

"Nobody who ever really looked at me would buy me an orchid."

"I suppose it's because I have to leave you at half-past four you think I'm just filling in time." I was ashamed, trying to explain and justify myself. "It was a man I telephoned, and he's coming for me at four-thirty. But I'm frightfully sorry, I've cut clean into your afternoon without even stopping to ask if you'd anything else on."

"It's a good thing you didn't," she said, her small, pointed face sparkling with sudden merriment.

"Why, had you?"

"I was supposed to be meeting a young man at the Redfern Gallery and then we were to have had tea together and probably gone to a movie."

"Whyever didn't you say so?"

"In the Catchment Board we learn to make quick decisions."

We were outside her flat door. I put my hands on her shoulders. "For better for worse, you're a nice child and I've enjoyed myself even if I have wrecked your day. Will you speak to me the next time I don't know you?"

Her face stiffened and she wouldn't meet my eyes. "No," she said quietly. "I'm damned if I will." And she closed the flat door gently in my face.

Three minutes later I was greeting Mandrake and letting him into the flat. He was large with disappointment. The Sitting Hen hadn't so much as a vacant hook from which he could sling a hammock and there was no other hotel in the neighbourhood.

All the bounce went out of me. Not very hopefully I said at last, "I suppose your friend Mabel Grey wouldn't feel like putting us up?"

"Good heavens, no. She's the busiest woman I know and the most overworked. She's a Member of Parliament, you know, besides the broadcasting and all the voluntary jobs she takes on for lack of anyone else to do them. I wouldn't insult her by asking her to waste her time on us. What about your Pritchard woman?"

"You think it's all right to insult her?"

"Well, if you're trying to arrange a lecture tour for her, it's fair enough; you needn't tell her we're interested in her murderous possibilities."

98

"As a matter of fact, she did offer to have me for a couple of nights, but . . ."

"Couldn't you bring a friend?"

"Well, yes, she said I could, only you see . . . there was something rather sinister about cats. The cottage is overrun with them."

"As if that made any difference. Can't you phone her or send her a wire?"

Of course it wasn't the thought of the cats that had deterred me, but the fact that I didn't want to be tied by courtesy to anyone's house and not free to follow my own devices. But you might as soon have tried to make water flow backwards as turn Mandrake from his purpose once it was definitely formed. Mandrake telephoned an elaborately worded and highly courteous telegram, dictated a note for me to leave for Brady and shepherded me out of the flat to a back street where he succeeded in buying a haggard but large-framed fowl, alleged to be a roaster, for much too much money and no questions asked. Then we took train for Barrow Lock.

CHAPTER NINE

At Barrow Lock we left the village where the river sparkled between steep banks and turned along Bogart's Way, which we assumed to have been named before rather than after Humphrey, and then past the telegraph poles and along a rutted lane called Edgar Street. Miss Pritchard's cottage was the first past the oasthouse. A huge tortoise-shell cat slumbered gently on the window sill. As we opened the gate and went up the path a telegraph boy got off his bicycle. Mandrake pulled a bell which made no apparent sound, and in the hush that followed we could hear, faintly and afar, the furious tapping of typewriter keys. The telegraph boy took his stand behind us on the path. Mandrake rapped with his knuckles and, after another pause during which the typewriting continued unabated, pounded the door with his fist. At last he lifted the flap of the letter box and roared through it a thundering "Yoo-hoo."

The typewriting ceased. A voice cried shrilly, "Yes, what? I'm coming." And presently the door was opened by Miss Pritchard, wearing a long, loose grey coat and skirt, no stockings, ankle socks and muddy plimsolls. The tortoise-shell cat streaked past us and in through the door to wreathe round her ankles, while a couple of tabbies from inside dashed out and began wreathing round ours.

"How do you do?" said Miss Pritchard a little vaguely, starting to shake hands and then seeing the telegram boy. "Oh, excuse me. Do come inside." She took the telegram and stood aside for us to enter, then picked up a letter and a paper slip from the mat. Holding them in one hand, she opened a door with the other and ushered us into a low, quite cheerful room, where two more cats aroused themselves and a cloud of dust from the sofa and came hopefully towards us. "Do sit down," said Miss Pritchard. "I remember you now. It's Mr. Crane, isn't it?"

"And Professor Mandrake," I said. "Miss Pritchard."

"How do you do?" said Mandrake. "It's so good of you to have us."

Miss Pritchard's mouth dropped open. She fell on her telegram and tore it open. Then she gazed at the slip that had been on the mat; one of those slips the telegram boy leaves when he can't make anyone hear.

"Oh dear," she said, "when I'm working I never hear anything. He must have brought the telegram and taken it away again."

"I'm dreadfully sorry," I said. "I suppose it's frightfully inconvenient."

"Oh no, I'm delighted to see you. Please don't mistake me. If only the shops weren't shut."

"With remarkable foresight," explained Mandrake, "we obtained a bird on our way down. I shall be more than happy if you will allow me to cook it."

"Will you really?" said our inadvertent hostess. "Oh, then that's splendid. Is it teatime? Shall I get you some tea?"

We assured her that teatime was long past and that we had had it. She offered us cigarettes and then said, "I'd better do something about beds."

"Simon will help you," said Mandrake hospitably. "I shall retire to the kitchen if I may, with the bird."

He dislodged a grey and a cream-coloured cat from his knee, where they were devotedly investigating his parcel, and stood up. Miss Pritchard led him to the kitchen and made him free of the pots and knives, and then I followed her upstairs. While we sorted linen and blankets I embarked on several literary conversations that should have been down her street. I asked if she worked to a definite plan of so many hours a day or just haphazardly, and she said, "Oh, definite hours—at least that's what I intend. I start about half-past eleven, or twelve, or sometimes four or five, and just go on until I'm hungry or the machine sticks or I wear a hole in the ribbon. No, I must have been wrong about the definite hours. Pull your corner a bit more. There's too much sheet my side. I'm giving your friend this bed. Do you think it'll be wide enough for him? Ought we to pull it away from the wall?"

We pulled it away from the wall. A confused mewing broke out in the garden and I looked out of the window to see Mandrake, in a cloud of cats, furtively pulling out a root from the vegetable plot. It proved to be the wrong root and he tried to put it back.

"Do you make a great study of crime?" I asked as we started on the second bed. "Do you read up famous cases and go to the police courts a lot?"

"Good gracious, no."

"Where do you get the ideas for your murders?"

"From life. Look, you're treading on the pillowcase."

"But surely you can't know a lot of murderers?"

"I know a lot of people who ought to be murdered."

"Isn't it rather dangerous, putting actual people into stories?"

"It would be if I did. But when I come across someone who seems to be asking to be done in, I try and re-create the basic reason in a new set of characters and circumstances."

The ash from her cigarette cascaded over my sheet and she stooped to sweep it off onto the floor.

"Do you read a lot of detective stories?"

"Oh no. They bore me to tears. You see, I'm not interested in the regular tough guys and killers, and I couldn't write about them anyway. Murder only begins to interest me when I feel I could have done it myself."

She turned the sheet back from the pillow in a businesslike way and started to lead me downstairs. I said, "Doesn't that tend to make you feel too much sympathy with the criminal?"

"I always do," she agreed. "Even in the cases I come across in newspapers I find I'm identifying myself with the criminal, seeing his point of view and understanding exactly how it happened and how impossible it is, afterwards, to explain or justify a course which at the time must have been inevitable."

Eight cats were outside the kitchen door which Miss Pritchard opened to reveal Mandrake, bending over a huge iron pan on the stove, poking with a wooden spoon at a sizzling, slightly blackened mess from which came a powerful smell of onion. The bird lay partially dismembered on the table, and two of the cats detached themselves from the kneading and prowling horde and were instantly on the table.

"Who opened that door?" boomed Mandrake, laying about him with the wooden spoon. "For the love of heaven, use a bit of plain horse sense and keep them out of the kitchen."

Miss Pritchard and I scooped up armfuls of cats, and withdrew while he drove the rest after us and slammed the door, cursing horribly.

"Now there," said our hostess interestedly as she led me into her study, "is a case in point. Your friend, I do not doubt, is the soul of courtesy in all his customary dealings. Yet, maddened and frustrated to this pitch, he becomes a very demon. Magnify the circumstances, make the man an eminent chef, say with an important banquet at stake, let him have been infuriated and thwarted at every turn and finally, just as he is getting to grips with his task, let some malicious person let loose the cats—and there's your motive and your murder and your murderee."

"But surely you can't visualise yourself doing murder in such circumstances?"

"No, but change the circumstances, translate them into something nearer one's own heart and temperament, and you soon would have a murder into which you could enter with insight and enthusiasm. It would be useless for me to tackle a murder halfheartedly."

She was collecting scattered pages of typescript as she talked, and stacking them into a pile which became the only neat thing in the wildly disordered room. When she had moved the lid of her typewriter and a couple of books from the least occupied chair she suggested that I sit on the chair. She was on the point of putting the lid on the typewriter when she stopped and asked if I understood typewriters at all. I rashly volunteered to do what I could.

"It's the ribbon," she explained. "The thing that switches it over from the top half to the bottom doesn't work. I've given up trying to use it, but it means that the top of the ribbon gets worn into holes and the bottom half wasted. I wondered if there were any way of reversing it so that the top came to the bottom."

"Only by taking it off the spools and rewinding the ribbon upside down," I suggested, "and that would be no end of a job."

"Oh, never mind, then." She looked disappointed. "I'll tackle it some other time."

Since she put it like that, there was nothing for it but to try. Gingerly I withdrew the right spool and began to unwind it, trying not to get ink all over my fingers, but in vain. I found it impossible to wind it back onto the spool tightly enough without gripping the ribbon firmly, and the other end wrapped itself round my feet or my wrists or my neck, to the infinite enchantment of the younger cats. In the corner of the room the tortoise-shell was growling darkly to itself over a raw limb of chicken, and everything that wasn't inky was dusty and it all seemed to cling to me. I was getting very hungry, too, and though the aroma from the kitchen grew richer and more penetrating, there was no further sign from Mandrake.

At last I had the ribbon fixed and inserted a sheet of paper. "I think it's all right," I said. "Just try it and see."

She sat down and tapped feverishly for a moment. "That's fine," she said. "I always write the oddest things when I'm testing the machine. It probably throws sidelights on my subconscious if we only knew. I'm getting hungry, aren't you?"

"Oh, not desperately."

"I don't suppose I've had anything since breakfast. When I stop working I get the cumulative effect of the whole day. But I daren't go near the kitchen, dare you?"

"Not like this, anyway. What I'd really sell my soul for is a wash."

She led me to the pump outside the back door. "There's only this or the sink," she explained. "We'll boil a kettle, if you like, as soon as your friend sounds the All Clear."

I got as clean as I could with cold water in the dipper. "Don't tip it away," said Miss Pritchard. "I'll use it too, and then I must empty it over the garden. We're having a drought in England, if you know what that means."

I didn't.

"Five fine days and nights in succession," she explained and disappeared with the dipper. I went back into the study. A grey cat was approaching the tortoise-shell about the chicken bone. The atmosphere in the corner was growing tense. I tried to shoo them from the room, but their growls became alarming, so I left them to it. The test page was still in the typewriter and I paused beside it. "Who said, 'All Time's delight hath he for narrow bed . . .'?—That's what I said," she had written. It might have come out of Miss Pritchard's subconscious, certainly, but it had been somewhere else first. It was a bit of a poem by de la Mare that I had read many times. It was supposed to be an idiot talking about someone who had died, and who, the idiot seemed to feel, was happier so . . . only the real line was, I felt sure, "hath *she* for narrow bed," and Miss Pritchard had written "he."

She came in just as Mandrake emerged hot and proud and beaming from the kitchen. "There we are," he announced contentedly. "I'm afraid the man lied when he said it was a roaster. I've had to casserole it. But it ought to be good."

Miss Pritchard's face fell. "Good, yes, I don't doubt it, but *when?*"

"It'll be tender as a fledgling by nine to half-past," beamed Mandrake. "Say ten to be on the safe side." Full of goodwill to man, he flung himself into a chair and relaxed happily while two cats shot out, spitting, from under him.

"But didn't you say dinner?" I whispered.

"Well, you don't want to dine much before that, do you?" asked Mandrake. "I never do if I can help it. A casserole's got to be slow to be any good at all. You can't hurry it. What we all need now is a drink. Suppose we go out to the Sitting Hen while it's cooking."

I think Miss Pritchard would have preferred a little bread and cheese, quickly, in her own kitchen, but her personality couldn't stand up against Mandrake's. She retired to change her plimsolls.

"Has she got an alibi?" asked Mandrake briskly.

"I haven't the slightest idea."

"What in the world have you been doing all this time?"

"Trying to be polite and take her mind off your rudeness."

"Poppycock," said Mandrake. "I don't believe you suspect her at all. I can't imagine her making a record for your uncle. She isn't the type. I believe you've dragged me here on a wild-goose chase."

That it was a wild-goose chase as far as Miss Pritchard was concerned seemed perfectly sound, and I saw no purpose in pointing out that I couldn't have prevented Mandrake's accompanying me if I'd tried. It was true, too, that it was hard to connect Miss Pritchard's rather businesslike personality with the flutingly girlish voice that had made the Cynthia Spalding record. My mind was straying back to Marcia again, for outside the cottage anything might happen. Every turn in the lane might bring me to her. There was even the glorious possibility that she might be in the Sitting Hen.

Miss Pritchard joined us in brogues and a man's pork-pie hat and as we set out I began to enquire about her neighbours. She told me she hadn't the slightest idea who they were, since she seldom recognised anyone, nor indeed noticed people in the street except for very good-looking young men, preferably navvies and with red hair.

I said, "Isn't there a colony of intellectuals in the village?"

"I'm told so, but they wouldn't know me, you know, unless my books were printed on handmade paper and remaindered. I'm not down their street."

"But surely your poetry is," I said. "Oh, I don't mean it gets remaindered."

"It does," she assured me grimly. "But they don't know it's mine. I suppose Anstey told you?"

"I'm afraid so. I hope you don't mind. He told me my uncle Cyprian used to come to Barrow Lock a good deal for week ends."

"Yes, he spent a night at my cottage once," she added thoughtfully, "but the cats bothered him."

Mandrake gave a snort and I said hastily, "I never met him, you know." For I had learned by now that no one was likely to speak their mind about my uncle until I had established my own indifference to him. Then I said casually:

"Did you like him?"

"No—I don't think anyone did, except, of course, my cats. They wouldn't leave him alone, but they're notoriously bad judges of character. Or perhaps they just wanted to annoy him. Cats can be pretty cynical."

"So there was no love lost between you?"

"Love?" she said soberly. "Lost?" Her face hardened. "Cyprian was a cruel man. A ready-made candidate for murder, if you like. I've often thought I'd have to murder him sooner or later."

"And now it's too late," I said unthinkingly.

"Oh no. The fact of his being dead makes it much simpler. I needn't even disguise him. He can't sue me for libel and I don't suppose you will."

"My dear lady, it's the last thing any literary agent would dream of."

She said suddenly, "You know, I'm very glad you came. A young man like you must have much more interesting things to do. I'm only sorry I didn't get the telegram. It does seem stupid of me," she went on, "not to have any food in the house. You see, I have the rations delivered on Fridays to be sure there's something over the week end, so of course there's never anything at all by Thursday."

"They come on Friday *morning* or *afternoon?*" asked Mandrake, with a sudden sly glitter in his eye that told me he was after her alibi if she had one.

"Friday morning," said Miss Pritchard, and then recollected. "Well, not always."

"Did they come *last* Friday morning?" he persisted, but she seemed not to think there was anything strange in his interest and went on obligingly, "No, that was the trouble. It was four in the afternoon before I realised they hadn't been. I had to leave everything and dash down to the village. They told me the boy had brought them in the morning and couldn't make me hear so he'd taken them back again. As it happened, I hadn't been typing that morning, just correcting with a pencil, so I'd have heard him. I expect he'd just forgotten."

"Oh—ah," agreed Mandrake, making a hasty calculation whether Miss Pritchard could have murdered Cyprian at four and still got to the grocer's in Barrow Lock before it shut. I was making the same calculation and had decided she couldn't. Then again, I was thinking, we'd only her word for it, but that, too, had occurred to Mandrake. "Suppose I come in to the village and get them for you tomorrow morning," he suggested innocently, "just to be on the safe side?"

Miss Pritchard said, "That would be kind."

We were now in a cobbled street at the very edge of the river, with the lock itself ahead of us on our left and ancient, irregularly spaced buildings on our right; shops, cottages, a little church and finally the inn.

"Now the Sitting Hen," said Mandrake as we approached, "is a perfect example of paradise lost—the English local at its best and most dignified turned over to the English vocal at his, and, alas, her, loudest and least dignified; the intellectual pub. You will observe," he continued as he steered us through the main doors, "that the decent obscurity of the Four Ale, through which we are passing, is not for us. The presence of a woman in our party quite rightly disqualifies us. The door on the right, however, admits us to the Snuggery, where the difference between the sexes is neither so pronounced nor so irrevocable."

We were now in a low-roofed, raftered room into which a hatchway opened off the bar in the Four Ale. A few oak settles were round the walls and there was a fire burning although the evening was close and growing thundery. The room was crowded and the air was blue with cigarette smoke and heavy with apathy. We planted Miss Pritchard on a vacant settle and went to the hatchway for drinks. As we rejoined Miss Pritchard a youngish woman in corduroys and sandals called across the room, "Professor Mandrake. Hullo. Wasn't it awful! You must have been one of the very last people to see poor Cyprian alive."

The apathy lifted and most of the people in the room crowded in our direction, greeting Mandrake and one or two saying hullo to Miss Pritchard. The mention of Cyprian's name seemed to have revived them and they were eager to hear news of him.

"Yes, I daresay I was one of the last to see him alive," agreed Mandrake, "but Simon Crane, his nephew here, has it over me. He saw him dead."

There was a hush of reverence and envy, a nasty little shock of pleasure.

"It was so sudden," said the girl in corduroy trousers, "he was really quite young."

"Couldn't have been over fifty," said a suave, rather plump young man in a green silk shirt and beautiful flannels, "and at the height of his powers."

"I don't know about that," said a languid youth in sailcloth and sandals. "That type often writes itself *out* quite early. I think he was probably lucky to go out when he did, before the decline and fall."

"He didn't go out. He burned himself out," said a short, streaky-haired woman in a mustard jersey and ginger slacks, who somehow contrived to look like a leopard.

The pall of gloom that had been on the place had lifted and they made us their pivot, eager to show off, since their lion was dead, any evidence they could muster of their familiarity with him, to me, his nephew. They told anecdotes of his wit, his whimsey, his cruelty; stories against themselves and each other; but under all I could not but sense the furtive triumph that he, who could so easily outwit and humble them, was dead, and they, mice though they might be to his lion, were alive.

One man alone had remained aloof in the chimney corner, crouched over his beer with his face in shadow. Now he rose with his empty tankard and came unsteadily towards us. He was small and slight, but his eyes and eyebrows had such tremendous force under his shock of greying hair that from the nostrils upwards I shouldn't have been surprised if he had broken into prophecy then and there. But even the carefully tended reddish-grey beard could not disguise the weakness of the mouth and chin.

"So the Bearded Reedling has emerged from his dudgeon," said the plump man, but I knew already who he was. I had seen him before. He hadn't been sober then and he wasn't now. He was Marcia's uncle Stephen.

"It's a quare thing," he said, with the blank blue stare of a seer, "how empty this place seems now that man's dead. For if ever I hated anyone, I hated him, and I'll drink to his eternal damnation with any one of you."

CHAPTER TEN

"Just a moment, before you do anything worse," said the leopard-woman. "Stephen, this is Simon Crane."

"I've met you before," said the Reedling, gazing at me piercingly.

"I doubt it," went on the leopard-woman, "or you wouldn't be so eager to shoot off your mouth. He's Cyprian's nephew, so stop boasting about your terrible gurt hatred and behave in a civilised manner."

"Civilisation," said the Reedling, "now that's the curse of the age. That's why the death of a man like Cyprian leaves us comfortless. It's the rarest and most stimulating thing in the world to be able to feel a genuine hatred. It's the grit in the oyster shell that makes us produce our pearls."

The plump young man in the silk shirt placed his glass on the bar. "Is that what enabled *you* to produce *your* pearls?" he enquired disparagingly.

"And what made you a connoisseur of pearls?" flamed the Reedling. "You jobbing grocer of the literary world, you script-writer, you dialogue-gushing hot-water system, to run luke-warm at the snap of a director's finger? Just because you've sold yourself to the devil, just because you can buy an expensive round of drinks for every shandy we real men can afford—does that make you fit to judge so much as a well-planned dung heap?"

"Don't be a fool," said the script-writer. "You'd be in pictures with the best of us if anyone'd have you. You'd do any job they'd pay you to do."

"I would not," cried the Reedling. "I'd be boiled in oil before I'd prostitute my talent carrying out the sort of assignment that consists in writing a 'short, emotional scene full of suspense and human drama' between an orphan gangster and a mongrel dog that'll bring a sob to the throat of the two-and-ninepenny seats."

The script-writer signalled the landlord to fill his glass. "Does your wife take the same high view of your destiny, I wonder?"

"You leave my wife out of it."

"But can you *afford* to leave your wife out of it?"

"You're telling me I live on my wife, now, is it? Ah well, that's one insult *you'll* never have to put up with. It isn't blood you have in your veins but soda water. There's not enough positive good or bad or anything in you to rouse a life-sized hatred in a bedbug. Cyprian was worth ten of you——"

"Oh, come on, have a drink on me and forget it."

Regretfully the Reedling placed his glass tankard on the bar for the landlord to fill. "There you are, you see," he said bitterly, "you can't even carry a quarrel through to the end. You have to buy me a drink and all's square, and I, because of my terrible thirst, have to swallow my fine distaste for you and accept it." He gulped thirstily and then laid the tankard down. "Cyprian wouldn't have humbled a man like that. You could hate Cyprian to the bone and he'd not curry your favour. Why, Cyprian's whole value to the National Quiz was that whenever he opened his mouth he had everyone in the studio, as well as the listeners all over the country, so bristling with active hatred that they could have picked up the nearest missile and flung it at him . . . like this . . ." He grabbed the tankard, ready to throw, paused and emptied it in one swift swallow, then flung it, with violence undiminished by the delay, just past the ear of the script-writer, to smash against the overmantel at the end of the room.

"Sit down," said the leopard-woman. "You're stinko. Take things easy." The Reedling subsided onto the corner of the settle on my left.

Having dodged the flying tankard, the script-writer now

shrugged his shoulders with an air of dubious bonhomie and asked the group at our table what we would have.

"I'm not drinking anything," said Miss Pritchard in a strangely fluting voice which suggested she *had* been, "and I'll pay for myself when I do."

It was a gesture of odd dignity, from a partially drunk woman, and curiously enough it summed up the feeling of most of us in a sentence. If the Reedling, because of his infirmity, could not refuse a drink from his tormentor, very well then, we would refuse on his behalf. For no one could like the scriptwriter, while, in spite of the exhibition he had made of himself, it was impossible to dislike the Reedling. For all his beard and his greying hair, his slightness and fresh complexion gave him an absurd youthfulness, but despair had settled over him like a pall as he huddled in the corner of the settle.

"Why'n't you go home to Mabel?" asked the leopard-woman. "You're high as a kite."

"Mabel thinks I'm in Edinburgh," muttered the Reedling. "I had to do some business, so she bought me a ticket."

"Then why are you here?"

"I met some people and missed the train anyway. I put up with Andrew and meant to go on in the morning. But I missed that train too, so now it's too late."

"Why'n't you go home now?"

"No hurry," said the Reedling. "No hurry. Mabel'll be disappointed in me. Don't like to disappoint her before I need." He subsided into gentle slumber across the table.

It was then that I had the questionable idea of becoming the Reedling's best friend and taking him home to Mabel once he could no longer make it under his own power. I moved to the bar and ordered a round for our party, then I placed a fresh tankard of beer at Stephen's elbow and roused him.

"Better not go to sleep, old man," I said. "You might get turned out. Tell me why you hated my uncle Cyprian so much."

A flicker of animation came into his eyes at the sound of my uncle's name.

"Did me a harm," he answered. "Did me the greatest wrong one artist can do to another." He brooded a moment in silence, then noticed the beer at his elbow. "It's yours," I said. "Tell me about Cyprian."

He sipped slowly. "Fifteen years ago I was a young man of promise. Everyone said so. When I married Mabel, mine was a name to juggle with. I'd not done a lot, but everything had distinction—some verse of my own, an appreciation or two, one or two anthologies of other people's lesser-known works—but somehow or other my great book never got written though we were all always expecting it. Mabel expected more of me than anyone else at the start. I was such a wonderful talker." He smiled bitterly. "I still am. That was the trouble. When I got alone with pencil and paper I'd talked it all away and I'd nothing left to say. Mabel would come in where I was working and find nothing done and she'd be disappointed. I hated that, so I'd go out where I could talk and feel a man again. When I got talking I always knew I could do it and everyone said, 'Just wait till the Reedling gets down to it, we'll see something then!' People were still on tiptoe to see what I'd do when I really got going. Only Mabel had seen through me and stopped expecting anything. And so had I, I suppose."

He took a cautious pull at his tankard before he went on.

"Mabel's niece got left an orphan and came to live with us. My wife grew very fond of her, fonder than she was of me, I shouldn't wonder, and I got fond of her myself. She was a bright little thing and I don't doubt she was more rewarding than I. For the things she began to write found a market—just children's stuff at first, you know—and she didn't waste her time and my wife's money talking and drinking in pubs, oh, dear me, no. We hadn't any children, either, so they became everything to one another and I was the outsider. Mabel even stopped asking how my work was coming on. She took it for granted that it wasn't. That irked me too, though it had irked me before when I'd felt like a watched pot, with her waiting for me to produce my masterpiece. Mabel was standing for Parliament those days and I was beginning to look less and less of a thing. The day Mabel was elected Labour Member for Wrottesley, I knew it was the end. My wife was a Member of Parliament. I'd got to be something or nothing." He leaned forward, drained the tankard and laid it portentously beside him. "You'd never believe how it took me."

"How?"

"I was ill," he said. "I even thought I was dying. I had the feeling all the manhood had gone out of me into her. I suppose it takes a sensitive nature to know what it would mean to a man like me to wake up and know that his wife is a Member of Parliament."

He seemed to expect some confirmation, so I agreed with him that it was a state of degradation few men could appreciate without experience.

"But once the crisis was over, when I was still too weak to leave the house, I started to write. I went to work, white-hot, on the thing I'd always known I could do and I kept at it. It was my answer; my proof that I was alive. Once I was well enough to be out and about again, I'd come back here and have a couple of half glasses, never more, for now I'd got half a book on paper, nothing could have kept me from finishing it, and when I got back I'd go on. It was a work of genius and I knew it. I wouldn't say a word of it to Mabel; it had to be a surprise for her, but of course I had to talk to someone, so I talked to Cyprian, and Cyprian listened and fed me with questions and paid for my drinks, and he recognised it for what it was, a work of genius."

As he folded his arms across his narrow chest, and his eyes shone fire, I believed in him.

"Being a work of genius, it wasn't everybody's book, so you'll appreciate it took a little time finding a publisher."

"Naturally."

"The delay just made the difference. The day my book came out, Cyprian's own parody of the thing was published too; the two books lay side by side in the booksellers', they were reviewed in the same columns of the same papers, five lines for my blood and torment and the rest of the column for his piece of razor-edged satire on all those who take themselves and their destiny too seriously. He was too big to have done it and you'd have said it wasn't worth his attention. His name and his reputation and all his big guns should have been trained on something his own size, not on my one desperate bid against oblivion. But there it was. We were a nine days' wonder, he and I together, and then I was forgotten, or merely held as a collectors' piece to be kept on the shelf beside his volume to give point to its satire."

"What an extraordinarily petty thing to do."

"Well, it was and it wasn't." Somebody had filled the Reedling's tankard. He took a deep contemplative pull. "You see, Cyprian never had a creative idea of his own. He was dependent on new things coming up for him to destroy, and I suppose he was short of something to destroy just at that moment. In a way it was a compliment that he'd thought me worth the effort. It settled things for me, too. After that nobody could go around saying I hadn't tried. I'd tried and just been blasted off the earth. Nobody expected me to try again. At least I was free of the sense of responsibility for my own genius. I could settle down and talk or write an occasional piece of criticism without anyone feeling I was squandering the inner fire that should have been setting the Thames alight. It made me important in a different way. If Cyprian were in here when I came in, a silence would fall. People knew we were enemies and they knew why. We'd say a few things to each other and have everyone listening in an electric hush that would draw out the best in you. If there'd been a Boswell there, taking down, he'd have had a collection of pieces of verbal swordplay that would have put everything else in that line into the shade forever. We spoke with the tongues of men and of angels and we had not charity, no charity at all. We were the central figures in a hallowed feud whose tension never let up. Strangers coming into the Sitting Hen for the first time would be told about us, and would hope that we'd both be in that week end to exchange our insults. It was a splendid hate, based on a genuine outrage that you could respect yourself for resenting. It made me important. And now he's dead."

He reached for the tankard again and drained it wearily. Then his head drooped forward on his hands.

The evening was oppressively hot. Miss Pritchard's few drinks on an empty stomach had clearly gone straight to her head, so that the missing link between her and the Cynthia Spalding of the gramophone record was revealed. In her cups, Miss Pritchard was fluting and girlish and arch. She was engaged in an animated conversation with the youth in sailcloth trousers on the other side of Mandrake, so that she was leaning forward and talking across him. Mandrake tilted his head a little backward and inclined it to his left. "That bird should be just about right," he whispered to me.

"Look here, don't wait for me," I said. "I'm seeing Grey back to his home."

Mandrake looked at me in amazement. "I thought you were hungry," he said.

"So I am, but I can't leave the poor devil to sleep in the gutter."

"Somebody'll take him home. Who bought him his last drink?"

"I did," I lied. "It's my moral obligation to get him safe home to his wife."

"His wife?" said Mandrake thoughtfully. "Are you trying to invent an excuse to meet Mabel Grey?"

"No."

"No sane man would forego a casserole like that from mere Christian kindliness. There's something more."

In a very confidential voice I said, "Yes, there is something more."

Mandrake looked at the Reedling and then he nodded. "I see," he said. "The house is called Cedar Lodge. You won't have an easy time finding it. I'd come with you if it weren't for that casserole—and, of course, our hostess," he added hastily as she suddenly concluded her conversation and seemed disposed to take a hand in ours.

"Casserole?" she cried gaily. "Yes, of course. Let's go."

Mandrake explained my predicament over the Reedling and tried to hold up her departure long enough to give me a brief account of the route to Stephen's house, but Miss Pritchard was all for the road and had him out of the place in no time. "We shan't wait supper for you" were Mandrake's last words.

And now it was closing time and I was trying to get Grey to his feet. The script-writer, driven to a desperate bid against his unpopularity, offered to help me and to set me on the way, and lugging the Reedling between us, we set out along the main road, then branched off to the left and then left again up what was not much more than a cart track.

The closeness of the night now resolved itself into growl after growl of thunder, and the script-writer, whose goodheartedness, after all, couldn't be forced beyond reasonable limits, whisked his coat over his head and shoulders and fled back to the main road and shelter as the great drops of rain began. I hoisted the Reedling onto my back with a fireman's lift, and plodded on. It was easier going, and that way he got most of the rain.

It was a nightmare journey. One time I landed us both in a ditch and one time I lost a shoe and had to go back for it. I was becoming so acutely hungry that I could not prevent my thoughts from returning to Mandrake's casserole. But all the time, through the aching muscles and soaking discomfort, was the heartening conviction that they couldn't turn me out again into the rain and dark on a night like this.

The first house I came to was the wrong one and I was nearly eaten alive by a dog, but at last I came to the low, rambling house with an enormous cedar by the gate. I hoisted my burden higher onto my back, went up the path and rang the bell.

There was silence, then a light blinked on in an upstairs window, and I heard footsteps coming down the stairs and along the hall. The door was opened by a smallish, bright-faced woman with crisp grey hair which waved away from her face. She wore a long dark blue housecoat buttoned and belted, and the smile wavered off her face as she saw us.

"Mrs. Grey?" I said. "I've brought home your husband."

"Oh dear," she said. "Is he all right? Will you bring him in?" She switched on a light and stood aside for me to take him into a room.

"Perfectly all right," I said as I took him in. There was a settee against the wall. I laid him on it as comfortably as I could and stood up and drew a breath or two. "There's nothing the matter with him that a night's rest won't mend."

"Just drunk?" she asked anxiously. "He hasn't been run over or in a fight, has he?"

I said, "No, nothing like that. Shall I help you put him to bed?"

"If you would."

When that was done she said, "You're soaking wet. Shall I lend you some of his pyjamas and put you up for the night? You can't go out in this."

I followed her downstairs in silence, feeling horribly mean now that my plan had materialised. She gave me a pair of his slippers and took my coat and shoes. "I'll get you a hot drink anyway," she said. "Are you hungry? Shall I find something to eat?"

I felt suddenly sick and weak and ashamed. "I'm all right," I said. "I'll go home."

CHAPTER ELEVEN

It was the last thing I had meant to do. Then I felt, rather than heard, someone in the passage. Mabel said, "It's all right, darling, it's Stephen. Someone's brought him home. He can't have gone to Edinburgh after all." And there in the doorway, cool and imperious in a scarlet-and-white housecoat, stood

Marcia, while I huddled on the settee, soaked, mud-spattered and ashamed, just long enough for her to recognize me and for her lip to curl and her face turn to ice. Then I got to my feet and said, "Well, thanks very much. I'll be going now."

"Nonsense," said Mabel. "He can't go out in this. He'll sleep on the settee here, in my study. Find him a couple of rugs, Marcia, while I get him something hot. It's the least we can do."

If Marcia had been nice to me too, I doubt if I could have seen it through. I should have crept away, ashamed, but Marcia was brutal. "Hadn't you better get your shoes on again, if you're really going home as you say?" she asked, stinging my pride and awakening me from abashed humility to some semblance of fight.

"On second thoughts," I said, "I've decided to stay after all."

Of course you couldn't be dignified with wet socks and no shoes on, so I only achieved a sort of jaunty defiance, but it did me good.

"Do you want me to tell my aunt why you've come and who you are?"

"By all means, if you're certain of the facts yourself."

"I know you're Simon Crane. I can only assume that you've come here in an attempt to pin a murder on me . . ."

"Or?"

"Or to pester me . . ."

"With my loathsome attentions? As a matter of fact, I came to visit your aunt Mabel. What makes you think I knew that you'd be here?"

"Oh, you'd know. You're the boy detective, aren't you? You'd know where I was."

"Is that why you left town without a word to me, when you knew I was hoping to take you to lunch?"

"I never promised to lunch with you."

"No, but you would have promised if I'd pressed you to, before I gave you back—your property."

Her eyes looked through and past me. "Didn't I understand

you when you told me that you never intended to try and barter it for anything I might possess?"

"You understood me. But I'd imagined even you couldn't be totally without generosity."

Her face grew suddenly bitter with self-contempt. "You shouldn't have let your imagination run away with you. I'm not what you think. I'm nothing like the woman you could care about. I never give anything. You'd have done better to trade the records for whatever you wanted than to act chivalrously and throw yourself on my chivalry. Go away. Smash that picture in your heart of me and leave me alone. There's nothing in it for you."

She closed the door quietly behind her and my eyes travelled round Mabel Grey's study with its reference books and neatly stacked papers, pens in the pen tray and violet ink. In about five minutes Mabel came in with folded sheets over her arm and carrying a tray on which were scrambled eggs and a pot of tea. She set the tray on the table and placed a chair for me. As I took my place she said, "Oh, Marcia forgot the rugs," and, opening the lid of the ottoman on which I'd been sitting, brought out two travelling rugs.

"It was good of you to bring Stephen home," she said. "You mustn't think too badly of him."

"I don't," I assured her. "I like him."

"He gets so disappointed," she tried to explain. "And then he thinks I shall be disappointed, and he tries to put it off."

"He's been telling me about himself."

Her chin went up. "If he told you he could have been a genius, he was right," she said. "Sometimes I think it would have been all right if he'd married a different woman."

"What sort of woman?"

"I've always been so distressingly brisk and practical. I work to plan and carry everything through as I've intended; not brilliantly—I don't set myself impossible standards of perfection like Stephen—but competently. I'm adequate and tidy and self-contained; one of those appallingly businesslike people who answer letters by return of post." She turned to me almost pleadingly. "Can't you see how disastrous that might be to someone of a totally different kind?"

"Surely not, if he were strong enough."

She turned away as though it had been too much to hope that I should follow her reasoning. "Oh, nobody's suggesting that Stephen is a strong character," she said, "but there are other qualities, equally valuable. It's silly to try and explain, I suppose. Only sometimes I've felt that if he'd been married to someone kind and rather helpless, not a very good manager and even perhaps a bit stupid, it might have worked out better."

She was making up my bed on the ottoman and slipping a cushion into the pillowcase. "Even my niece, who used to live with us, turned out definite and rather successful and hadn't much time for him. There's never been anyone normal and un-ambitious whom Stephen could outstrip and leave standing." She laid Stephen's pyjamas on my pillow. "Better women than I have subdued their own personalities and devoted their lives to making a success of husbands no better than mine. I suppose I was too selfish."

"Or too honest?"

"Honest?"

"Yes, surely. And you had too much to do that could be done by no one else."

"Had I?"

"You must know you had. But for an honest woman you've made out a wonderful case against yourself."

She laughed softly. "I'm sorry. I suppose I was a bit off guard. Making a forlorn attempt to justify myself—or Stephen —to a complete stranger in the dead of night. And even with your mouth full and someone else's slippers on, you're putting me at my ease and making me feel useful and necessary and good. You're a very nice young man. Would you like to tell me who you are?"

I would have told her anything. What was worse, I felt sure I was going to. "I'm Simon Crane," I said. "But besides that, I'm a total fraud."

"Are you really," she asked cheerfully, "or do you just feel it's your turn?"

"I didn't bring your husband home out of kindness at all. I did it because I hoped I'd be asked to stay the night."

"Do you mean—you planned it—got Stephen drunk on purpose?"

"Hardly that, though I did buy him one drink, but I was darned glad of the excuse to bring him here."

Her face had hardened. "Why?"

"I'm in love with Marcia."

"Good gracious." The hardness went from her face and she almost laughed. "But where do you come from?" she asked. "How did you happen to be about?"

"I came down from town on the excuse of seeing Miss Pritchard, who's a neighbour of yours, because I believed Marcia would be here. I was in the Sitting Hen this evening, trying to figure out some way of getting to know you, when I saw your husband and thought of this idea."

"I see." She paused a moment, then shrugged her shoulders. "Well, it came off. Why are you throwing in your hand?"

"Because you're so nice."

She stood up. "Oh well, now you've got that off your chest, I hope you'll sleep as well as can be expected on this ottoman."

"Aren't you angry with me?"

She smiled. "Stephen's my husband," she said. "I'd much rather have him brought home even on false pretences than not. If you'd been really hardened you needn't have owned up at all."

I said, "Maybe I'd better get everything off my conscience at once. I'm Cyprian Druse's nephew."

It was a moment before she spoke and then she said, "And why is that on your conscience?"

"You and he didn't get along."

"You mean he made me look like a sentimental fool on the air?"

"He tried. And you made him look like a disgruntled old satyr. I never met my uncle," I added. "That last recorded quiz programme was the first time I ever heard his voice. Did it give me a fair picture of him?"

"You mustn't ask me," said Mabel. "I can't help being biased. We both had our backs to different walls."

"I don't mind telling you all my money was on you."

"Oh dear," said Mabel, smiling. "What a responsibility. I do hope you haven't got a lot of money." She moved towards the door but stopped halfway. "Does Marcia know you're in love with her?"

"Yes. She hates the idea."

"You shouldn't have told her. Marcia only likes difficult things."

"I'm pitifully easy."

"Go to bed. I'll think of some advice for you in the morning. I've never embraced a cause yet that wasn't lost before I found it."

"Are you going to embrace mine?"

She stood a moment in the doorway, sizing me up with her kind, amused eyes. At last, "I still think you're very nice," she said, with an upward inflection which suggested she was as surprised about this as I must be. And then she left me alone. I peeled off my sodden clothing, spread it over a couple of chair backs, put on the Reedling's pyjamas, which came midway down to my shins, and went to bed.

I wakened to the wild thrill of bird song that no one had told me was the most noticeable feature of an English country morning. I climbed off the bed, pulled back the curtains and wondered how the heck I should find the bathroom. As I reached the door I saw a slip of paper sticking under it. It said, "Bathroom first left top of stairs. Lavatory straight through kitchen." I availed myself of the information and found a man's dressing gown hanging on the banisters. Mabel really was invaluable. I should have hated to run into Marcia with my shins exposed.

I went back to bed, but now I couldn't sleep and at half-past six I gave up the attempt and decided to dress and go for a walk. In the kitchen I found my shoes, placed carefully on trees, with my coat on a hanger, near, but not too near, some species of British boiler. I put them on and let myself out by the back door, which was unlocked, into the sparkling, rain-washed world that seemed to have been born that instant under the just-risen sun.

I went round the house and out through the gate. The lane I had come by stretched away downhill, rutted and deep with pools. Uphill it was drier and led in an easy curve to a group of towering elms on the brow of the hill, which must have been a landmark for miles. Thinking that I should just make the distance and back in time for breakfast, I set out for them with a feeling of discovery. For this was an aspect of England I had not guessed at, and this was the place where Marcia had been a child.

Flowers bloomed in the ragged grass where once she must have walked and larks twinkled in the sky like inverted stars, spilling the rapture that was too big for so tiny a thing to contain. I thought of the long-legged child growing up, knowing every bird and tree, and I wondered how she could have borne to go away—and how she could have borne to come back to such a place, if the thing I feared had happened—and I knew that she couldn't. No, if you had murder on your hands, even a justifiable murder, surely you would have stayed among crowds, in the towns, where nothing was altogether real in any case, rather than step out into such a clean-washed morning where you could not choose but come face to face with your maker, or at least with yourself.

As I walked, with this feeling of exaltation possessing me, I realised that there was someone already under the elms. I remembered that the back door of the Greys' house had not been locked, and my heart leapt at the thought that we had both been driven out under the same compulsion to find the same goal. It seemed that all differences and defiances must melt from between us at a touch and we should fuse into blinding light. I did not stop to consider that she might equally well strike me across the face for interrupting her privacy, as I strode swiftly forward, feeling like the son of the morning, watching the woman in the long green coat.

I was approaching silently along the grass verge and she stood, with her shoulder touching the great bole of a tree, looking straight ahead, with her back to me, but now she turned a little and I saw that it was not Marcia but Mabel. I ought to have known which of the two of them would be likely to be up at this hour; only, of course, I had not assumed Marcia to be there from habit, but from some divine compulsion urging her to a heaven-planned tryst with me.

I was nearly upon her now, and I kicked a stone so that it rattled along the lane, for you might come upon the woman you love, unawares, if you cared to take the risk, and all fair, but it was not fair to creep thus upon a stranger.

She turned and her face was lovely at that moment, with a look of infinite sadness and infinite compassion. She held out her hand to me and I took it and stood beside her in silence while the great trees darkened the sky and shuddered and murmured above us. The feeling of the permanence of infinity seeped into me, along with the sorrow of our impermanence, which is the prerogative of trees and high places. After a long time she said, "It should be Marcia, not me."

Of course that was what I had been thinking, so I didn't answer. She said, very gently, as though she were explaining to a child that the rainbow didn't end anywhere, "It never is, you know."

"Not Marcia," I said, "you mean, for me?"

"No, I didn't mean that. I mean it's never the real person. Never the person we think of, who should be sharing this splendour and this silence. Don't demand it. Don't expect it. Whoever you live with and love and enjoy, you're always alone in your moments of vision." She looked beyond me with inexpressible sadness and loneliness. "If the other person really existed or could ever exist, we should have no need to die."

She spoke so abstractly that I told myself I didn't understand her, but I felt what she meant, though in my heart I was vehemently rejecting it all the time. It might have proved true in all its implications for her, but for me, if I could have Marcia, it mustn't be true.

There was nothing I wanted to say and we said nothing, just stood under the towering elms, with the earth dropping away on all sides in green slopes, to the valleys and towns and railway lines and men. Then both in one instant we turned and went back down the lane towards her home.

CHAPTER TWELVE

We walked in silence for some time, then, "I ought to be asking you how you slept," said Mabel, "but it's perfectly clear that you didn't, so I won't. I'll lend you Stephen's razor while I get breakfast. Nobody else will be up for ages."

While she fried bread and tomatoes and made coffee I shaved over the sink in the kitchen, feeling more at home than I had ever felt with anyone. We breakfasted together on the yellow checked cloth on the kitchen table and soon, as I hoped, she began to talk about Marcia.

It was clear she had loved the child deeply and had watched her grow and helped her unfold as though she had been her own daughter. It was clear, too, that the absence of children was the main tragedy of this unsatisfied household. Mabel didn't speak of it, but it lay unspoken between us throughout the meal. Presently she said, "Of course I know I failed in some way with Marcia or she wouldn't have gone. Not that I tried to stop her. People have to develop in their own way, and perhaps she couldn't do it here. I expect I was too fond of her. It irks some people. It isn't fair, either. You lay a burden on them and the fact that they can hurt you is the most unfair of all."

"Has Marcia hurt you?"

"Oh no," said Mabel hastily, "I didn't say that. She's always delighted to do anything I ring up and suggest, and charming when we meet for lunch, but I've never been to her flat and she almost never comes here. Of course it's perfectly all right so long as she's happy and doing what she wants to do. People go through stages when they have to break away from everything and find themselves. Only I keep getting the feeling that she needs someone else to find her."

"And you think it could be me?"

"It would be very nice if it could. Have some more coffee," she added hastily, "if you're prepared to regard the brew in this pot as coffee."

Marcia came into the kitchen in a lilac-and-white silk print, a townswoman dressed for the country. She looked pale and extraordinarily fragile against Mabel's uncompromising tan, but there was a gleam of humour in her eye as she said, "Good morning. I suppose it was too much to hope that you two wouldn't get on like a house on fire. Has Aunt Mabel been showing you my first tiny shoe?"

"The first time you set foot in my house you were wearing size thirteen Wellingtons," said Mabel firmly. "I may have been lacking in sensibility, but I'm afraid I didn't preserve them. We're having fried bread and tomatoes. Will you cook your own or shall I?"

"I'll cook my own," said Marcia, slicing tomatoes into the pan.

"I'm afraid there isn't any bacon till I fetch the rations," said Mabel.

"I'll go in and get them this morning," said Marcia, and added, as I opened my mouth to say I'd come with her, "I'd be glad of a walk on my own."

She smiled in the confidence that she had disposed of me for the morning.

"But I wanted Simon to do the shopping," said Mabel

briskly. "Men get on so much better. People think they're help-less and are kind to them. You'll have to wait for him outside the shops."

I didn't expect Marcia to take this lying down and she didn't. "Mr. Crane will have to be getting back to town," she said, turning her tomatoes in the pan.

"Will you?" asked Mabel. "I hope not."

"Well, not to town, in any case," I explained. "I'm staying with Miss Pritchard. Mandrake's there too. You know him, don't you?"

"Yes, of course. I see him every week at the National Quiz. Oh well," she went on cheerfully, "if Miss Pritchard's got him she can't need you as well. Let me see, I've got my secretary coming, so I shall be busy all this morning. I shan't want to see either of you. Suppose you do the shopping, then go round to Miss Pritchard and make your peace with her and then, if she'll let you, come back to lunch at one."

It seemed an ideal arrangement. Mabel found the ration books and a basket and made a list while Marcia ate her breakfast.

"How long have you had a secretary?" asked Marcia.

"Quite a time now. It's too bad that I've got to work while you're here, but if I don't put a little dynamite into this housing scheme people will be raising their children in the hedgerows. There's so little time," she said, looking suddenly harassed and older. "I've got to find someone to do some typing, too. I suppose you don't know of anyone?"

She turned to me and I shook my head.

"Can't the secretary do it?" asked Marcia.

"There's too much for her. She barely gets through the letters and dictation in her time. Besides, she's only a child. This has got to be accurate."

"I believe I do know of someone," I said suddenly. "Brady said my uncle had just sent his last manuscript work to a Miss Tangent; she's bound to be accurate because my uncle was pernickety in the extreme."

"She sounds ideal," said Mabel. "Here's the list for Mrs.

Pledge. That's the grocer. Marcia will show you. The question mark at the bottom is to remind you to say, 'And anything I haven't thought of?' and look trusting and hold the basket so she can slip some salad dressing or anything into it without the other customers noticing."

"Somebody had my razor," said a dolorous voice in the doorway. Stephen stood there, dressed but unshaven, looking like an accusing minor prophet, blinking in the sunlight. My chair was behind the door, so for the moment he didn't see me.

"You took it with you to Edinburgh," said Mabel. "Dear knows where it may be now."

"In the waiting room at King's Cross, where else?" said Stephen reasonably. "But ye have a spare one we bought at Woolworth's for just such a contingency: I keep it in the bathroom cupboard and it's there no longer."

"It's on the draining board," said Mabel.

"And what more natural?" he inquired with fine sarcasm. "No doubt my dressing gown has been cut up and hemmed for dishcloths?"

"No, darling. I lent it to the young man you brought home last night."

"Is it a young man I brought home now?"

"It is," I said hastily, getting up to shake hands. "I'm Simon Crane. Good morning. Your wife very kindly put me up for the night."

Stephen had nothing but pleasant memories of me. "So it's you?" he asked, wringing my hand. "I'm glad to see you. You were saying some penetrating things last night about Cyprian Druse." He put an arm round my shoulders as though he had personally discovered me. "Mr. Crane is a thinker of insight, my dears," he assured his womenfolk, "and a talker of power. And good morning to you, Marcia," he added pointedly. "It's a rare thing for you to be up so soon in the morning, surely?"

Marcia seemed to have withdrawn both in body and spirit. "I'm just off to the village to get the rations," she said, clearly between the devil and the deep sea.

"I'll come with you," said the Reedling.

"But you've had no breakfast."

"Breakfast. I want none of it."

"Just a cup of coffee, anyway," said Mabel, hastily pouring a cup.

"Well, just a sip maybe, but no more than a sip."

He sat down at the table while Mabel swiftly spread butter and honey on a slice of bread and put it within his reach. Marcia ran her fingers down her shin and said softly, "I've laddered my stocking. Damn. It's my only pair."

"Take a pair of mine," said Mabel.

"No, that I won't," said Marcia. "Can you lend me something to mend it with?"

"There's a basket on the window sill by my dressing table. If you'll bring it down I'll do it. Couldn't you go without on a day like this?"

Marcia shook her head solemnly. "No, darling, I'm not the type." As she moved to the door I observed with surprise that she really had a ladder in her stocking. "Don't wait for me," she added. "I think I won't come to the village after all. You'll be able to go on with that powerful and penetrating discourse without interruption."

Stephen watched her resentfully as she closed the door. "Is it poison I am?" he asked.

"No, I'm poison," I reassured him. "She never intended to come at all."

Stephen was at once on my side. "And what's wrong with you, I should like to know?" he asked belligerently, emptying his cup with characteristic thoroughness. "Come on, then." He got to his feet with the folded bread and honey in his hand. "She'll not find us sitting here to plead with her when she comes down." He moved out into the passage, picking up a wide-brimmed dark green hat and a stick, flung open the door and ushered me from the house.

I was glad to see that his previous night's experience sat so lightly on him. His step had the briskness of a boy's and his eye a child's innocence. So little of his face would, in any case,

have come in for a shave that the lack of it did little to spoil
his grandeur.

"My wife's upset with me," he confided as we walked. "And
so's my niece. I'm best out of the house for a bit. Is it true I
brought you home?"

"In a manner of speaking. We brought each other."

"I can remember nothing of the matter. I was drunk, is it?"

"It is."

"Ah, it's then a man learns who is his friend." He forded a
pool in the lane. "It was raining, maybe?"

"It was."

"Was I—walking a little or did you carry me on your back?"

"You weren't walking very much."

"It's a fine thing to be a strong man in the fearless pride of
his youth." He walked on, deeply thoughtful. "But we'd met
before last night, hadn't we now? Don't tell me. I shall remember in a minute."

In that case, I thought, we might as well get it over. "I threw
you out of Marcia's flat a few nights ago," I said.

"There now. I knew I was not mistaken." His satisfaction at
being proved right seemed quite unclouded by any resentment,
while his admiration for my fearless youth had increased. "But
you say she has a poor opinion of you, nonetheless?"

"No opinion at all, so far as I can see."

"Women are unaccountable."

It was then that she caught up with us, walking quickly and
without a hat. "I changed my mind," she said. "I remembered
something I had to get in the village."

She fell in beside us, but the track was too narrow for three
of us to walk easily abreast. Stephen said, "I'll drop behind.
That's fair enough. Simon can talk to you and look at your face
while I'll watch the beautiful rear action of you for consola-
tion."

She winced, said, "I'll walk at the back myself," and
dropped behind.

"I'm a clod, do you see?" said Stephen, loudly and elaborately behind his hand to me. "Everything I even look on is

polluted by my foulness. And her with no stockings on at all, nor suspenders even, to mar the lovely liquid line from the buttock to the heel."

It was then I withdrew any allegiance I might ever have felt for the Reedling. I turned my head for a moment and saw that Marcia was blushing miserably. No, you couldn't take that sort of thing from your uncle, even by marriage.

I threw him a conversational cue and let him talk to the air while I busied myself with the problem of how I could get rid of him and talk to Marcia on my own. It did not occur to me that Marcia was busy with the same problem. As he led me into Pledge's grocery store, she caught me by the wrist. It was the first time she had ever touched me, and I should not have been surprised if the skin had come away in her fingers, her touch so shocked my system.

"I'd like to speak to you when you come out of here," she whispered. "I'll be in the stationer's."

Speech was beyond me, so I returned her pressure and followed the Reedling into the shop. Mandrake was at the counter, cat hairs clinging to his dark suit, with Miss Pritchard's ration book and shopping list. He had greeted me as an ally returned from reconnoitring in enemy country before he noticed the Reedling, but the Reedling evinced no curiosity.

As he turned back to Mrs. Pledge, Mandrake's voice took on a note of guilelessness that should have warned the most unwary. "And Miss Pritchard said, as she has visitors staying, could you possibly let her have a bit over the ration?" I watched him in alarmed admiration as he went on doggedly, "It's hard enough to manage on one book at the best of times, and last week she took her rations early—on the Thursday was it or the Wednesday? So naturally there's nothing in the house."

So Mandrake was after her alibi, only he'd played his hand too well.

"There's not much of anything to spare this week end," grumbled Mrs. Pledge. "And strangers about, too. I've had one or two come in with emergency cards. I don't like to disoblige

Miss Pritchard, but there's nothing I can suggest except perhaps an extra couple of ounces of cooking fat. She could rub you up a little tart with that with some rhubarb out of the garden," she suggested, brightening, and nothing more would she yield.

"But"—Mandrake returned to his pitch determinedly—"we were having a sort of wager about who could stretch out their rations longest. Just to settle the question, could you remember which day she did get her last week's rations?"

"Oh, if Miss Pritchard says it was a Wednesday, Wednesday it was."

"But she said it was Wednesday *or* Thursday."

"Then Wednesday or Thursday it was. Miss Pritchard wouldn't tell a lie."

"It was in the afternoon," persisted Mandrake, looking, from the back of his neck, very hot. "Don't you close either of those afternoons?"

"Yes, we close Wednesday. Then Thursday it must have been."

The affair was concluded for Mrs. Pledge, but not for Mandrake. "But *was* it? I really must make sure."

A modest queue had formed behind Mandrake and me, and popular feeling was beginning to run high, but Mandrake was not a man to be lightly intimidated.

"Sid," called Mrs. Pledge in an exasperated bellow, "what day did Miss Pritchard 'ave 'er rations last week? Gentleman 'ere says 'e 'as to know."

A languid boy wearing bicycle clips appeared in the back door. "Dunno," he said. "I took them round Friday arternoon and couldn't get no answer, so I brought them back."

"So she fetched them herself later on Friday afternoon?" asked Mandrake.

"Suppose so," said the boy. "I wasn't behind the counter, Friday, but they was gone next time I noticed."

"When was that?"

"Saturday about midday."

Mrs. Pledge washed her hands of Mandrake and started

attending to me, leaving Mandrake's little mound of groceries on the counter for him to collect. We worked through my list, and when I got down to the question mark, I threw everything I could into the appeal, feeling that my reputation with Mabel depended on it.

"I haven't done much shopping since I've been over here," I said, trying to look gawky and like Gary Cooper, and probably succeeding in looking gawky. "So if there's anything I ought to have asked for, and haven't, will you think of it for me, ma'am? I don't want Mrs. Grey to scold me."

Mrs. Pledge's heart went out to me. I feel sure that she felt I might almost have been her boy, trying to make his way in a strange land.

"Why, yes," she said, "of course. There'll be soda, washing powder, soya-getti and a tin of beetroot." She propelled four wrapped packages into my basket as she spoke, and then, leaning heavily on the counter, wrote the actual names of these last four purchases on my bill. They proved to be gingernut biscuits, corn flour, salad cream and a tinned Canadian Christmas pudding. Whatever Mabel might feel about the haul, it was clear that I had something Mandrake hadn't got.

Mandrake was waiting outside the shop with his ill-gotten cooking fat in his hand. "That gets us nowhere," he grumbled. "All we know is that she might have been in London on the afternoon in question and she might not. Why couldn't you back me up?"

"A shopping queue of housewives isn't the best place for making delicate, unobtrusive enquiries."

"I thought asking for the extra rations would make her suspicious and she'd tell me Miss Pritchard had her rations on the usual day and send me about my business."

"Leaving the impression that poor Miss Pritchard was trying fraudulently to obtain extra cooking fat."

Mandrake regarded his parcel mournfully. "She seems to have succeeded. What am I going to do with it?"

"Put it in with her other rations. She'll never notice a bit that size."

"A woman not notice two ounces of cooking fat? You don't know England."

Stephen joined us as Mandrake started to put it in my basket.

"Let's send it to Mabel," he said. "She's sure to be glad of it."

"Send what to Mabel?" asked Stephen.

"These two ounces of cooking fat," said Mandrake.

"Does your own household require no cooking fat?" asked the Reedling with dignity.

"No," said Mandrake flatly.

I had been trying to think of something that I needed in the stationer's and now hit on the idea of taking Miss Pritchard a gift of typewriter ribbons. It was clearly just what she would appreciate and might soften my past churlishness in deserting her all night and my future churlishness in deserting her for lunch. Mandrake said it was a hopeless quest, and he was pledged to wait in the fish queue anyway for cods' heads for Miss Pritchard's cats, but Stephen thought that, with so many literary pygmies in the vicinity, the shop was sure to carry a stock. He obligingly accompanied me down the road, but as we started to cross towards the stationer's, I mentioned that Mandrake had been telling me what an admiration he had for one of the Reedling's early publications, and how he considered it one of the greatest works of promise of its generation. This succeeded admirably. The Reedling courteously excused himself at the door of the shop, retraced his steps and was lost to sight in the fish queue for a considerable time.

I joined Marcia in the stationer's, where an assistant was indefatigably demonstrating a new type of fountain pen which would write in any position, except, it appeared, the one in which you happened to be holding it at the time. I bought two red-and-black ribbons, one blue and one plain black, which was the entire stock at the moment. While the man was wrapping them, Marcia drew me behind one of the bookshelves which made up the lending-library half of the shop and said, in an intimate voice, as though we had known and been able

135

to count on one another for years, "I've got to get back to town this evening. Can you be on the six thirty-five?"

CHAPTER THIRTEEN

"I—I can't," I said, so startled that I stammered. "I've got to spend *some* time with my hostess."

"Then why not go back to lunch with her? Make your peace and get your business done and catch the train up with me. Then I'll explain." There was sincerity and urgency and no mockery in her eyes.

"Mabel's asked me back to lunch with all of you."

"She's too busy to have you really. She won't mind if you don't come."

"I'm sure she will."

"Why?" She spoke sharply.

As before with Marcia, I could invent nothing. "She thinks I'm such a nice friend for you."

"Very well, suppose I think so too? Be on the six thirty-five and we'll have dinner together in town, if you'd like that?"

"Of course I'd like it."

"Then smother Miss Pritchard in charm and typewriter ribbons and professional zeal and she'll part with you without a murmur when the time comes. Will you?"

"Of course."

"She'll probably want to sleep a bit after lunch. If she does and you feel like any exercise, I shall be walking along the ridge past the end of your lane somewhere about half-past three. There's a bit of old Roman wall that you oughtn't to miss."

"I wouldn't miss it for anything."

With Marcia's fingers just touching the sleeve of my coat,

my feet never touching the pavement and my heart acting like a caged squirrel, I crossed the road and went with her into the Sitting Hen, where we found Mandrake and the Reedling. Still in the same mood, I had introduced Mandrake and Marcia before the stiffening distrust on his face reminded me that Mandrake imagined I had come to Barrow Lock to investigate Miss Pritchard's alibi, and that Mandrake was also the person to whom I had confessed I was in love with Marcia. From the distaste on his face it was clear that he was now seeing through me in a quite large way. Even so, I could not feel discouraged or ashamed.

There had been no cods' heads to be had, though the fishmonger had admitted to one box of fish as yet unopened, which might contain anything. I at once suggested I should join the queue myself, determined to go to any lengths, even halibut, rather than that Miss Pritchard's cats should suffer unnecessary privation. I asked Marcia to come with me but she said no, she had wanted to meet Professor Mandrake for years and she meant to make the most of her opportunity. Mandrake's face did not soften.

The box proved to have held mackerel, so I compromised with a couple of those and then bought a large bunch of sweet williams from the greengrocer, so sincere was my intention of being utterly delightful to Miss Pritchard for the brief time I was to be hers. The morning had grown very hot. On the road back Mandrake maintained a brooding silence, but nothing could depress me, and even when I opened Miss Pritchard's gate and observed that her own garden was already overrun with sweet williams, I consoled myself with the theory that it is the thought that counts.

Miss Pritchard was charmed with the mackerel and deeply touched when I offered to put a new ribbon on her machine. It was almost gilding the lily when I insisted on washing up after lunch. I discussed the coming publicity campaign from every angle and even suggested that I comb some of her cats while she read aloud from an unpublished poem, and presently, quite casually, I asked if there were a good late-afternoon train. She seemed quite willing to let us go and Mandrake said nothing at all, having fallen asleep. By a quarter past three Miss Pritchard was yawning in the heat as she darned innumerable ankle socks. I stood up and stretched. "Do you feel like a walk?" I asked, holding my breath for fear she should say yes.

She considered the proposition. "Do you know, I really think it's too hot," she said apologetically, "if you'd forgive me. Last night was rather late for me and I'm not used to late nights."

The sun blazed and no wind stirred. The poppies and columbines, revived by last night's rain, were wilting again as I went up the lane to my tryst. And even as my heart sang at the thought of meeting Marcia, here in the summer's loveliness, I heard Mabel Grey's voice saying, "It never is, you know . . . never the real person. Don't demand it. Don't expect it. You're always alone. . . ." But Marcia was waiting for me, looking like a mondaine wood nymph, and the sight of her made nonsense of all that. She took me along a field path to a little hollow and we sat down where the Roman wall cast its shadow on a bank that was springy with thyme and misted with harebells.

The larks sang loudly enough to drown the thump of my heart but they couldn't hide the way a grass blade seemed to jump against my wrist, so I put my hands behind my head and rolled over on the grass. When she realised I wasn't going to talk she said, "Why did you come to Barrow Lock?"

"I thought you knew."

"I always think I know everything." She smiled disarmingly. "You tell me."

But I was determined that whatever came should come from her, so I said, "I thought it was time your aunt Mabel and I got together."

She said, "Oh—I see," as though she saw a great deal more than I did, and added slowly, "And what is friend Mandrake doing here? Is he playing cops and robbers too?"

"He doesn't believe Cyprian's death was an accident, if that's what you mean."

138

"It's exactly what I mean. Am I his principal quarry too?"

"You surely don't imagine I've said anything about you to anyone? Mandrake happened to be at the flat when one of the girls came to try and get her record back. With that and a few other things, he jumped to his own conclusions. He wanted to hear the other records but I wouldn't let him. That was partly the reason I gave yours back to you. I had to be sure it was safe. But when he decided to come to Barrow Lock with me he didn't even know you were here."

"And you only came to make my aunt's acquaintance. How one can flatter oneself. What do you think of her now that you've met her?"

"I've never liked anyone so much in so short a time."

"Never?"

"You're not supposing for one moment that *liking* is the feeling I have for you?"

"No?"

"No." I spoke the word harshly.

"You've got a lot against me, haven't you?"

I didn't answer.

"I suppose, for one thing, you can't understand why I've been so damnably ungrateful to my aunt. I doubt if I can explain it to you. In my own way I'm terribly fond of her. She's given me a great deal, quite apart from a home and education. I'm not a demonstrative person and I can't bear other people to be demonstrative, but I wouldn't have hurt her the way I did for anything—only——"

"Uncle Stephen?"

"You've worked it out for yourself." She turned on her elbow. "I suppose you'll always work things out for yourself. If I tell you anything at all, shan't I have told you too much?"

"Have you ever thought of trusting me? I'm sure it would save you trouble in the long run."

She met my eyes for a moment.

"How long is the run likely to be?"

"There's only another three weeks before I go back. I can keep it up if you can."

139

"What do you want me to tell you?"

"Go on about Uncle Stephen."

"I suppose it's obvious enough—to everyone but Mabel, anyway. It started when I was no more than a schoolgirl with him just teasing me, pulling my pigtails, rolling me over on the grass; it passed as an avuncular sort of humour, although I never mistook it for a moment. Even before I knew what it was about he made my flesh creep. But I could handle it then. Most of the time I'd be away at school, and on holidays I could run, I could hide, when he tried to wrestle with me I could even fight back. Sometimes I hurt him more than he let anyone guess, but it was supposed to be a game between us and Mabel never thought it was anything else. When I grew up it got worse. There was nothing I could do while she was present that wouldn't expose him to Mabel for what he was. Of course I saw to it that he never came near me while she *wasn't* there, but he always took advantage of her presence to stay as near me as he could. It wasn't as though he even went out to a job. He was always there."

"It sounds like a nightmare."

She turned and looked at me. Her eyes were deep and unhappy. "There was only one thing I could do, short of wrecking any bit of happiness Mabel had preserved for herself, and that was to get away. As soon as I could earn a living, I did. There wasn't always all of a living, either, but somehow I managed, and lately it's been better. In fact, I'm reasonably successful."

"And Mabel just thinks that you wanted to go and live on your own?"

"There was nothing else to tell her. She'd put everything into me that should have gone into the children she never had. I think I left her pretty high and dry except for her career. She's certainly made a success of that. I think she'd rather have just been humdrum and happy with the right sort of husband and children. As much as I could, I cut off from them altogether, for fear of it starting all over again. If he came to my flat, as he did, I could throw him out and no harm done. She wouldn't know. She told me he was on his way to Scotland, or I shouldn't have come down here this time. That's why I must get back this evening. If I don't he'll do something to make me flare up in front of her, and if that once happens she'll have to face the fact of what he's been trying to do all these years."

"Are you sure that would be worse than what she has faced?"

"Wouldn't it?"

"I think she's fonder of you than she is of him."

"But to have stuck to a man all those years, and borne with his drinking and boasting and failing, because he needed you —because you were all he'd got—and then to find he'd let you down in such a detestable way—wouldn't that be the last humiliation?"

"I don't know. It might be a good thing to have the facts in the open."

"But what could she do? She couldn't turn him out like a dog. Mabel wouldn't, anyway. Could she go on sharing house with him and loathing him every minute of her life? Oh no. Things must stay as they are and I must stay out of it."

"You may be right, but she's terribly fond of you."

Marcia's face was hard. "People have no right to be fonder of you than you can be in return." She looked darkly down towards the valley where the river flowed and her voice acquired a sort of impersonal anger. "I hate knowing I can hurt someone—that the way I talk or act or feel can affect someone who can't affect me. People have no right to make you responsible for their happiness."

"We don't do it on purpose."

"I didn't mean you," she said with a half apology. "I'd forgotten." And she looked unhappy.

"I shouldn't have reminded you. I'm sorry."

"But there's a sort of accusation in the fact of anyone being fond of you. It makes me feel accursed. I've never been able to bear it."

"Except from Cyprian."

She winced. "I shall never know what Cyprian really felt

for me or anyone. But he never pleaded, never humbled himself, never blackmailed you with his 'suffering' or his 'need' of you or his loneliness. He was every kind of cad. There's nothing to be said for anyone who lost their head over him, but at least no one could say they gave in to him out of pity; and if anyone was hurt, it wasn't Cyprian."

"I can't imagine you losing your head."

"I did worse. I lost my sense of humour."

"That isn't difficult when you're young."

"Only I've never been young."

"I was finding excuses for you."

"It's fairly easy to do that. He was the big boy on our paper. He scarcely ever came near the office, but you couldn't ignore him. Wherever I went I was asked about him, although the first time I saw him was at a private party after I'd been on the paper for a year. He brought me a drink, asked what I thought of the Picassos at the Tate and got me talking about my job. After a while it dawned on him that I didn't know who he was. At first he thought I might be pretending, to make an impression, but when he realised that after all that time on the same paper I hadn't found out what he looked like, he had to make an impression, himself."

"He succeeded." It was not a question and I dare say it was bitter.

She smiled wryly. "He used precision tools. Besides, it was such an extraordinary change from the sort of emotion I'd had to contend with before. I'd had more than my share of that blackmailing kind of affection—from Mabel, though she didn't mean to—the crawling humiliation of Stephen—then in the office there'd been a quite pleasant, gay young man on the society page who'd made me laugh over morning coffee most days of the week till I'd realised how much time I was wasting and stopped having coffee. The next time I noticed him he wasn't gay any more, just haunted and hangdog, with a look in his eyes that suggested his death would be at my door."

"Did you revert to morning coffee?"

Her face imperceptibly hardened. "What was the use? It

wouldn't have made the difference to him and I couldn't afford to waste time."

"Aren't you wasting time now?"

Her eyes dilated for a second, then her lashes dropped and she blushed. I said rather harshly, "You don't by any chance like me, Marcia, do you? That couldn't be why you're wasting your time with me?"

She took off her hat and leaned her head against the grass bank without opening her eyes. When she spoke it was scarcely above a whisper. "Why don't you find out?" she said.

So I kissed her among the thyme-scented grass and the harebells and learned nothing at all except that I was hot and clumsy and inexpert and her lips were firm and cool and cruelly sweet. I said, "No, I don't think you like me at all," and my heart thumped me reproachfully for letting it accelerate so sharply to so little purpose.

"But I do," she protested coolly. "I think you're sweet."

"Be damned to that," I cried, suddenly angry. I put one hand behind her shoulders and the other on her throat and I kissed her until she was breathless and shaking and taut. When I let her go she lay quite still among the outraged harebells. The colour of her eyes had deepened and her breath came slowly. She stood up and began to walk back along the pathway in silence. A few hundred yards above Miss Pritchard's cottage, I said, "I suppose you won't be on the six thirty-five after all?"

She looked down the valley, unsmiling, and wouldn't meet my eyes. "Oh yes," she said. "I shall be there."

CHAPTER FOURTEEN

When I got Mandrake onto the six thirty-five he was still inclined to be hurt with me about Marcia's presence in the town at all. The fact that she had been at the Greys' house and the possibility that this had influenced me into taking the Reedling home tended to shake his faith in me altogether. In the circumstances I thought it best not to mention that she was leaving on the same train, and it was just as well, because she didn't.

There were three people on the platform, and as the train came in and still she did not come, I racked my brain to find excuses not to take the train after all, but I had already taxed my ingenuity past its prime, inventing reasons why we should. I was as disgruntled as Mandrake by the time we steamed away.

Let me set it on record that the six thirty-five from Barrow Lock to Waterloo, though listed correctly as doing the journey in just under forty minutes, makes the slowest, weariest and deadliest journey in the history of man. Mandrake only spoke once, when he said, "Your friend Marcia Garnett takes a keen interest in your movements, doesn't she?"

I had been wondering what they had talked about in the Sitting Hen that morning, but now I replied angrily, "I doubt it."

"Oh, but she does," said Mandrake. "She was wondering how your work permitted you so much time to go wandering round the countryside, and how soon you would be leaving England again. I explained that you were a rather high-standing amateur member of an American bird-watching society, with a particular interest in the behaviour of bitterns, and that a bittern had been reported to have raised a clutch of little bitterns near Barrow Lock. I must say I got the impression that she didn't believe me, but then, alas, not everyone has the same trusting, not to say gullible, nature that I have."

That said, he folded his arms and sulked for the rest of the journey, while I watched the landscape as it spread itself between me and Marcia, and kicked myself inwardly for having been fooled again, and tried to rid my imagination of the feel of her in my arms.

When we reached London he said, "And now you've got me back a day sooner than we planned and I shan't be expected. Really the least you could do would be to give me dinner."

Being in the same situation myself and having no wish to go back to the flat, I was quite willing to give him dinner. Towards the end of the meal he began to expound the theory that the trouble about murder—as with childbirth—was that it was largely practised by beginners; that they made all their prentice blunders and learned their lessons over the actual murder that mattered. The scientific, though seldom-tried, approach, he considered, would be to experiment first on a comparative stranger whose death would not benefit one at all. Thus the initial clumsiness, the unpredictable, purely nervous reactions which might affect the murderer's behaviour before and after could be assessed at a time when the absence of motive ensured the minimum risk of apprehension, providing a store of experience to be drawn upon when the actual premeditated crime was to be committed.

"It seems sound enough, up to a point," I agreed, "but I don't see its bearing upon childbirth."

"It's clear as day," said Mandrake. "A first baby is spoilt, flatulent, difficult to rear, a prey to all the disorders in the infant-welfare manuals and reduces its parents to wrecks in its first year. Second, third and fourth children are invariably happy, thriving, well-mannered and content. The parents' strangeness, terror and anxiety has yielded to assurance. The parents *expect* the baby to survive. Now consider"—Mandrake leaned forward confidingly and poured himself a second cup of coffee—"the few murderers we *know* about—who have survived their initial crime—mostly wife-murderers—have usually gone on to a long and successful series of further murders, gaining poise and dexterity with each attempt. Again, take into account all those who have so perfected their methods by continued practice that we have never heard about them at all."

I could see that the field for conjecture was limitless and, to break his train of thought, called for the bill, but he was not to be deflected.

"Suppose for the sake of argument that I were to murder you, the law would look for a motive. Who had cause to wish you dead? Had I? Clearly not. I should be the last person on whom suspicion would fall."

"I wouldn't be too sure of that," I said hastily. "Quite a number of people on the station and in the train would remember the extreme irritability of your manner towards me today."

"Would they?" asked Mandrake, a little disappointed. "Possibly. Yes, I should have concealed that. Thank you for mentioning it. Everything has to be taken into account. Though that a trifling and justifiable irritability, such as I may have displayed, would amount to sufficient to throw suspicion on me, I wouldn't be sure."

"Still, just as well to begin the experiment somewhere else, don't you think?" Then I added, "Of course you might have murdered Cyprian without a breath of suspicion attaching to you, and be having a wonderful time taking me on a wild-goose chase after innumerable silly women while you laughed your head off."

"Why, so I might," agreed Mandrake in a voice of happy appreciation of his potentialities.

Presently he suggested we turn in to a news cinema we were passing. I had no reason to hurry home and agreed that we might as well.

As we groped for our seats a commentator's voice was saying, "But Druids are not the only people to have been involved in a period of great activity. Nearer home, the indefatigable members of the Housewives' Legion . . ." His voice faded as a large, voluble and expensively overdressed female figure invaded the screen, thumped some sort of banner-draped wayside pulpit and announced in refined and deadly cockney that though it was against her nature to push herself to the fore, since she hated doing anything "ostentious or conspicious," she felt it her "duty as a woman to protest against the Government's mishandling of public funds in the matter of food subsidies . . . and look at tomatoes . . ."

"Look at this one," cried an eager male voice, and a tomato smashed with gratifying accuracy right across the open mouth under its ridiculous, beflowered and tulle-veiled hat.

Considering it couldn't have been rehearsed, it was a beautifully timed and executed shot, and I was lost in admiration till well on into the procession of decorated bicycles in Brightsea's summer carnival before the words *"ostentious* and *conspicious"* detached themselves from my subconscious and rang the bell marked "Lisle Street Drab" in my memory.

That voice, that combination of mispronunciations, that hideous refinement, grown so much more opaque now there was so much more need to hide, that monumental respectability could only have flowered out of such a background and into such an environment. My uncle's acquaintance of the pavements must be a mayoress at least and doubtless an admirable one.

I asked Mandrake if there had been anything to show who the woman was, and he said, "No, why?" I explained in a whisper that her voice had been among my uncle's records. He began asking questions excitedly till people behind became restless and even asked him to be quiet. After that he made only occasional grunts, and jotted savagely in his notebook, while we sat the programme round until it reached the place where we had come in.

There was no indication of the woman's name or status, but from the pulpit on which she banged depended a banner with the strange device of "Hooper's Cross Women's Legion." That was enough for Mandrake, and as we stepped into the street his face was alight and all traces of his previous disappointment in me had been wiped away.

"So this is the woman you dismissed as unimportant?" he cried. "Then why in the name of thunder did you rely on your own judgment? She's obviously of some importance in her own horrible social stratum, and if the facts of her association with Cyprian were disclosed, or even of her previous profession, she'd clearly have a great deal to lose."

"I didn't know, how could I, that she'd moved up in the world and become a pillar of the Housewives' Legion?"

"It was your business to find out," said Mandrake, his anger at my incompetence warring with delight at his own perspicacity. "We don't know her name, of course, but Hooper's Cross should be sufficient to start our enquiries. I think," he added, with sudden, unlikely deference, "that you might leave this angle to me. I'll let you know the moment I have anything concrete to go on."

I was content to make him a present of the mayoress of Hooper's Cross, and left him in the highest spirits while I, lonely, forsaken and befooled, made my way back to Cyprian's flat, feeling that I had been beaten on a nerve by invisible rods and jeered at by invisible violins, all just a little off the note.

But why, I kept asking myself, had she made me kiss her in the thyme-scented grass among the harebells, if she had meant to treat me like this? And even while I asked, I knew the answer. She meant to be rid of me. To get me on to the London train and away. Marcia had no use for me, and as I stepped into the lift I registered my mental vow that she was rid of me, now and forever, though how and when I should be rid of her tormenting and humiliating image it was harder to say.

Inside my door was a small folded note. It would be from Marcia. Obviously it had to be from Marcia and it would explain everything.

It read:

I came up to say good-bye but you weren't here. I go
at the crack of dawn. I hope the real girl was nice to you.
HAZEL

I had forgotten there had ever been such a person, and she was going, had almost gone, back to the deadly boredom of Steeple Tottering, and I should not see her again.

Oddly enough, the thought of London without Hazel, now that Marcia was being brutal again, was emptiness, whereas, of course, if Marcia had really been on the train and had dinner with me, I shouldn't have noticed if the rest of the population had vanished. In any case, I had to say good-bye to the child. Back of my mind all along had been the intention to take her out again before her holiday was over, and try to give her something a bit more memorable to cheer the long watches of the Catchment Board, if it were only a matinee or a few shared jokes or another double ice cream and pie.

I considered ringing her up, but it was after eleven. Hazel wouldn't, I felt sure, mind being waked, but her sister might and her sister was sure to answer the phone. In fact, I might never get around to speaking to Hazel. I decided to scribble her a note and take it down and push it under the door. I wrote, "Whatever time your train leaves, please come up and bang on my door before you go—Simon," and went downstairs, making no sound on the carpeted treads and passage. I turned the last corner as Mrs. Best's flat door opened and Hazel came out in her dressing gown and put a milk bottle beside the door. When she straightened up and saw me, the wan little face grew so radiant that I had the utmost difficulty in not taking her in my arms.

"Did you have a nice time?"

"Not very," I grinned. "She let me down."

"Oh, I'm sorry. She probably did it on purpose to try and pique you."

"No. She just didn't give a damn."

"Poor Simon."

"What time is the crack of dawn?"

"Half-past seven."

"You can't *have* to go on that train."

"I do."

"No. No Catchment Board expects you back at midday on a

149

Saturday. You could stay up and lunch with me. You could even go back on Sunday."

"I'm expected at home."

"You could wire. We could go to a musical show . . . or, no, at your time of life a rather intellectual play, quite possibly by Sartre. Wouldn't you like that?"

"I mustn't . . ."

"Or a ballet? Something to remember in those long winter evenings when the romance of the Catchment Board is wearing thin?"

Her face crinkled into laughter. "If you put it like that, there's nothing else I can do. I begin to feel I owe it to my grandchildren."

"That's a girl. What shall we do?"

"Oh, anything," she said happily. "As if it mattered."

I felt a sort of stab at my heart. Again I wanted to kiss her, but instead I patted her firm little cheek in what I hoped was a grown-up way and said, "I'll call for you at half-past nine. We'll do everything."

I walked upstairs thinking some rather profound things about the Irresponsibility of the Life Force and found a folded note from Marcia on my mat.

> SIMON [it read], I'm desperately sorry. I tried to phone you twice this evening. Can we lunch together tomorrow? I'll phone in the morning at half-past nine and explain everything.

The northern lights were dancing for me again and the celestial choir in full song. She would telephone me at half-past nine. I had forgiven the life force and forgotten its irresponsibility. Then I remembered I should have left the flat by half-past nine and that lunch with Marcia was out of the question since I was committed for the whole day to Hazel. I knew that if Marcia spoke to me and convinced me that she hadn't let me down on purpose, somehow my promise to Hazel might dwindle to nothing, and, whatever other folly I might permit myself, this mustn't happen. Of course, I reasoned, I could ring

Marcia before I left and give her a chance to explain—yes, come to heel at the snap of her fingers, or a little before, like the guileless, clumsy dog she took me for—or I could pretend that I'd never had her note. I could say to myself, "Why in thunder can't she fulfil her obligations, or find some way of letting me know she couldn't, as everyone else would have done, as I would have done to her? And if she can't, let her take the consequences. Let her ring and find me gone."

And that's what I did. The telephone started to ring next morning just as I was letting myself out of the door, and I told Brady not to answer it. Let it go on ringing unanswered, as it was bound to ring in my head for the rest of the day, though I hoped to heaven I should succeed in keeping the sound from Hazel's ears.

CHAPTER FIFTEEN

Myrtle Best let me into the flat. She was determined, I am sure, that I shouldn't reproach myself for never having followed up her gesture of friendship with the Grade A milk, and made me sit down, while she told me the tension was beginning to tell on me, living so close to Cyprian's extraordinary presence. I pointed out that it was, in fact, his absence with which I had become involved, and she peered closely into my eyes and said yes indeed, the strain was beginning to be apparent, and that she knew a wonderful psychoanalyst if I should feel the need. Then Hazel took a firm hand and carried me off.

We saw the sculpture in the Park and did a river trip up the Thames. At lunch at Hampton Court, I said, "Tell me about your grandchildren."

"What grandchildren?"

"The ones to whom you owed it not to miss an experience like today."

So she told me about her grandchildren and I had to admit they were delightful. There was even a tentative couple of dark ones, since, she explained, by then we might have had another war and you had to allow for anything. Then she asked me about my grandchildren, and for a moment I felt a queer sort of pang that they couldn't by any alchemy be the same. She saw the sudden look of loneliness on my face, and put her hand on mine.

"Oh, I'm sorry," she said. "Things have gone a bit agley over your future, just at the moment, haven't they? Are you sure it wasn't a mistake? About the girl letting you down. I can't see why anyone would mean to. I expect she's sorry now."

And foolishly I said, "Oh, she is."

"You've seen her since?"

"No."

"Spoken to her? She's rung up or written?"

"She sent me a note."

"She is sorry and it's all all right? She's explained everything?"

"She always explains everything."

"You don't believe her?"

"I don't know what to believe."

"Has it been going on a long time?"

"As long as I can remember. Over a week."

"Perhaps she's in some sort of jam."

"Perhaps she is."

"Then you can't really form an opinion, can you? All you can do is to help as much as you can and make up your mind later when conditions are normal."

"Take all the kicks and run back every time she whistles?"

"Isn't that what you *want* to do?"

Of course it was. I recognized it instantly. I said, "There's a little matter of pride."

"Good heavens, man, you can't be in love and still talk about pride. Are you telling me that you've had a note from her

152

making peace and you haven't accepted it, because of your *pride?*"

"No. No, it wasn't that entirely. I suppose I'm a boob, but I'm not quite that sort of boob."

"Could it be that coming out with me prevented you from accepting the olive branch? Would she have lunched with you today? She would, wouldn't she? Oh hell, and I've been boring you about my grandchildren."

Hazel's eyes on mine drew the truth out of my face without the least co-operation on my part. I couldn't lie to her and it wasn't necessary to tell the truth. There she was already in full possession of the facts and seeing the situation far more clearly than I was willing to admit it even to myself.

I said, "Look, child, you haven't bored me for a minute. I don't think you'll ever bore anyone. You'll always see everything the wrong way round, not from your point of view but the other person's, and sometimes you'll see more than is really there." I realised there was no going back, so I might as well go on. "I could have had lunch with that girl today, but I wasn't sure I wanted to. I've been in a state of hallucination for longer than I care to think of, and I wasn't sure that I didn't want to be de-hallucinated and have a chance to think clearly for a change."

"I don't think I'm a very good de-hallucinator. It needs someone with a strong personality. Someone like me would only make you think of the girl that wasn't there."

I said, without rhyme or reason, "I wonder if her grandchildren would be so nice as yours?"

"Well, I'm sure they'd be much cleaner and quite certain they'd all be white."

I said, "Oh yes, they would surely be white," and I added, "if any."

She gave me a sparkling smile. "That, at least, would be up to you."

"I'm not so sure." It was hard to explain Marcia in terms Hazel was likely to appreciate, and yet for some reason I wanted to. "She's quite different from anyone else. She doesn't like anyone to be fond of her; hates people who show their feelings; and yet she does feel things herself, but in an inward way."

"You seem to have swallowed an awful lot of propaganda," said Hazel, "and as it's perfectly clear you haven't been de-hallucinated, wouldn't it be a good plan to ring her up and arrange to take her out to dinner?"

"Oh no. I'm taking you to dinner and a show."

She gave me a wholehearted smile that had the sun and moon in it. Then she said, "But you can't do that in any case."

"I'm going to."

"No. In the first place, you can't go to shows that you want to, in England, now, unless your parents booked the seats at the same time as they put down your name for Eton or Harrow. In the second place, I really am catching a train at three minutes to six, and this time it can't be altered. I've spent a fortune in telegrams and had value for every penny, but three minutes to six is zero hour and the rest of the evening is yours."

But I wouldn't ring up Marcia. We spent the afternoon at the Zoo, where Hazel extended her quota of grandchildren by a very small chimpanzee and a rather dilapidated bear. When I saw her onto her train her eyes were luminous. I asked her what colour they were and she said, "What do you suppose? They'd have to be hazel, wouldn't they? It's the dullest kind you can have."

"No," I said, after careful consideration. "They're not. They're the colour of mignonette."

"But mignonette isn't a colour. It's hardly even a flower; just a scent and a sort of memory from when you were a child."

"That's it," I agreed, "exactly."

"I was afraid of it," said Hazel. "It was nice, though, being bought an orchid once, even by mistake."

She was laughing, but I turned at once and ran down the platform and past the barrier, cursing myself for not remembering that she ought to be seen off with flowers, as well as the magazines that I *had* remembered. There was a kiosk with flowers and fruit and a few rows of horrid "Art" pots, and I'd found an orchid and even paid for it before the train steamed slowly, reluctantly but inexorably out of the station, taking Hazel away from me with no explanation of my abrupt departure, no good-bye and no orchid. And even as I stood with it in my fingers, watching the train, I knew that the chances were I should end by taking it to Marcia.

Mandrake was sitting rather bleakly on the floor outside my flat with a number of parcels. "I do wish you'd leave word with someone when you're going to be out all day," he said, getting to his feet. "I phoned you several times and at last I came along on chance. There's been someone else ringing, since I've been here. They've rung off, now, of course."

I unlocked the door and he preceded me into the flat. "I've found her," he said as soon as the door was again shut.

"Found who?"

"The mayoress of Hooper's Cross, of course. Not that she's actually the mayoress, but she hopes to be next year. I haven't spoken to her yet, but I've collected a lot of information. She's a simply perfect suspect. Whatever are you doing with that orchid?"

"Putting it in water," I answered firmly. "I like a few womanly touches about the place. What's her name?"

"Mrs. Umberleigh-Smith. I'm working on a scheme now that ought to reveal everything. If you'll sit still for a moment or two I'll explain it to you . . ."

The telephone rang. I said, "Mandrake, do you mind? I think this is going to be personal. If you could wait in the kitchen or the bedroom . . ."

"The bedroom will do very well," said Mandrake accommodatingly. "You don't mind if I have a look round?"

"Go ahead," I said, and snatched off the receiver.

"Simon?" The voice was nervous and unsure but it was still Marcia's. "I tried to phone this morning. You weren't in."

"Yes, I was."

"You didn't answer."

"No."

"Why not? How could you be sure it was me?"

"It was worth the risk." My voice was churlish and angry and hurt.

"You're so sure I couldn't have anything to tell you that you could want to hear?"

I couldn't keep it up. "Have you?" I said, too eagerly.

"Of course I have. Listen, Simon, when Stephen knew I was catching that train he decided to come up with me—to fetch his suitcase from King's Cross. There was no point in my going at all on those terms, so I called it off. Later I ran into some people I know who were motoring up at night. They offered me a lift and I took it without saying a word to Stephen. I phoned you the minute I got in, but you weren't there." She paused and I didn't answer. She said, "Simon, it's true. Don't you believe me?"

"I'm not sure I want to believe it."

"We were to have had dinner together last night. You could have made up your mind then how much you want to believe about me."

"But we didn't have dinner last night."

"There's tonight." The trace of uncertainty was gone. "Come and eat here with me. I'll expect you in half an hour."

"I—don't know——"

"Come and eat with me while you're making up your mind. I'll expect you. If you decide you don't want to know me, you can say so and we'll never meet again." And fearlessly, not waiting for my answer, she rang off.

Seeming too preoccupied to resent my departure, Mandrake followed me round the flat while I bathed and changed, asking me if I minded him staying on for a part of the evening and a host of extraordinary questions as to where the fuse box was and what I had done with Cyprian's small personal possessions which had been left to me. I answered him vaguely without really hearing him, decided to leave the orchid in the tooth glass and was at Marcia's door in exactly half an hour.

She wore black velvet with a scooped-out décolletage filled in with dark red roses and round her shoulders a scarf of fine black lace spangled with dark red and magenta sequins. The dress had a flamboyant simplicity, a sort of deliberate glamour that I should not have associated with Marcia, and as she opened the door to me there was an almost defiant gleam in her eyes while a trace of mockery curled one corner of her lip, though whether it were directed at herself or me I couldn't know. Even the lights were shaded and the wireless was mutedly playing some lusciously nondescript background music. My reason assessed the whole trick as I stepped into the flat and took the drink she offered, for I knew that this was a woman who'd keep her light definite, her outlines and her values clear-cut and her music good or silent, but my senses only told me she looked vivid and passionate and desirable.

I said, "This is nice," rather stupidly, and she said, "Is it?" and I noticed her hand was shaking. She said, "Shall you mind if we have dinner almost at once? I'm told there *is* a type of woman who can get a meal all ready and then ignore it with impunity for twenty-five minutes of unruffled badinage with her guests and no harm done, but it doesn't work like that with me. I'm not precisely a heaven-sent cook, but I can put over a wonderful bluff."

Avoiding the obvious retort by a hairsbreadth, I said, "I don't believe a word of that. I'm convinced you're a heaven-sent cook."

"You're not usually so easily convinced."

"Oh yes, I am, before the event. It's only afterwards I wonder."

We skirmished for positions, neither conceding an inch. Then when we had eaten she asked, "Don't you ever answer the telephone. Or have you been out the whole of the day?"

"I went out at half-past nine. Since then, among other things, I've done the sculpture exhibition, a river trip, Hampton Court and the Zoo."

"Never a dull moment," she laughed. "Were you having a wonderful time or just keeping out of range of the telephone?"

"Damn you," I said, getting up from the table. "I've never wanted to hurt anyone in my life before, but I'd give anything to be able to hurt you."

"And whatever makes you think you can't do that?" she asked. There was a newly lit cigarette in her fingers and as she stood up she stubbed it out. She turned a little towards me and stood quite still, with a pulse beating in her throat. I took her in my arms. She was just as a woman should be, curved and soft and yielding, taut and resilient, lovely to see and agonizingly lovely to touch, and as quenching to the thirst as the waters of a mirage.

At last she moved away from me and sank into a deep armchair. "Go on and hurt me, then," she said. "It isn't very difficult."

I snapped off the wireless's saccharine murmur and followed and stood over her. "You know I don't want to hurt you," I said. "You know far too much about me to be fooled by anything I may say when you goad me too far."

She stooped and took hold of one of her black court shoes. "Forgive me a moment," she said, "something's hurting my foot." She pulled off the shoe, slid her fingers inside and brought out something small and shining. For a second it lay on her palm, then her fingers closed swiftly over it, while with the other hand she slipped the shoe on again. "One of the crystal buttons from my sweater," she said, dropping the thing into her bag and snapping it shut. "I was afraid I'd lost it."

But I had seen it and it wasn't a button from her sweater. It was a crystal earring carved in the shape of a wing.

She turned back to me then as though it had really been the button from her sweater, as though this reminder of the horrible and violent death of my uncle meant nothing to her in this world, and, "As you were saying?" she said.

I had accepted the possibility that she was my uncle's murderess, and had assumed the circumstances to have been such that they would have justified her, if all had been known. I had deliberately refused to think about it in any great detail, but now, with her warmth and perfume in my nostrils and her softness and desirability taunting my senses, it was suddenly revolting and terrible that she should so lightly, so deftly explain

158

away the earring with a lie and turn back to me without a qualm to take up the embrace where it had been left off.

I said, "I doubt if I was saying anything as engrossing as Cyprian must have said to you a dozen times."

"But Cyprian's dead," she said, "and you're alive."

I put my fingers round her throat as she leaned backwards, half smiling, as though daring me to hurt her and knowing that I shouldn't. "Why did you do it?" I said harshly. "Tell me, for pity's sake. Tell me anything. I'll believe anything. Only make me understand. Make me know how it happened so that you couldn't have done anything else. So that I can love you and keep my peace of mind."

"What do you want me to tell you?"

"That you killed Cyprian."

"Even though I didn't?"

"That was the second earring in your shoe. The pair of the one I found on his settee under Cyprian's body."

"It was nothing of the sort. I told you. It was a button."

I tore the bag from her fingers by force and shook its contents onto her table. I pounced on the earring and held it before her face.

"Why, to be sure. How could it have got in my shoe? Perhaps it was planted," she went on, her face sobering strangely, "by someone who wanted to see me hanged by the neck until I was dead."

As she spoke her fingers hovered to her throat and touched it, as though she saw, as I saw, and as I agonisingly felt, the anguish of her soft loveliness jerking out its life at the end of a rope. I swept the soft, pretty muddle of her bag's contents from the table into my hands and flung them into her face, turned on my heel and left the flat.

CHAPTER SIXTEEN

Sunday was a wilderness. A dozen times I reached for the telephone to speak to her. A dozen times I started along the corridor to apologise; to tell her I had come to my senses and knew very well I had been mad. For one moment I saw clearly that no woman really guilty would behave as she had behaved; if the earring had been accidentally in her shoe she must have felt it sooner; she had put it there on purpose, meaning to find it when she did, to test me, or even to throw suspicion on herself in order to shield someone else. The next moment I would remember the half-light and the music and the deliberate assurance with which she had yielded herself into my arms, and then I would think, she was afraid when I followed her to Barrow Lock. She changed towards me then and became all gentleness, to get me safely on the London train and keep me here, where she could watch me and keep me blinded and bewitched till I was safely back on the boat and out of the country. Most of all it stung to think she was willing to humble herself and me to this, without an atom of affection for me, when all she needed to do was to stand aloof and tell me the truth, whatever it proved to be, knowing I should not hurt her or demand any sacrifice. Then I would begin to argue all over again that she was too proud and had already proved herself too courageous to have given herself unwillingly into my arms to save her skin. She had done it for someone else, or, if that were impossible, there were moments when I almost convinced myself that she too had been touched by enchantment and was in love with me as I was with her. But if so, why hadn't she trusted me as she must have known I was to be trusted and told me the truth, fair or foul, as to why the earring had been in her shoe? The trifling question whether she had in fact killed my uncle or not would have had no importance to me if she had only given me the wildest chance to believe in her on one ground or other.

I had noticed certain minor changes around the flat in the position of furniture and so forth, and indeed I had found a note from Mandrake on my return in the evening:

> Had to make a few alterations. Don't touch anything.
> I'll explain tomorrow.
>
> MANDRAKE

but there was nothing that inconvenienced me and I could not flog up the remotest interest in whatever he might be up to. Instead I found myself watching the telephone, which remained resolutely silent. As evening came I threw in my hand and was just going to telephone when the door buzzer went. I hung up and opened the door and found Mandrake. He came in beaming. "I've had a wonderful day," he said, flopping into a chair. "Nothing I did could go wrong. I'll tell you all about it."

He began to describe his thrilling pursuit and capture of Mrs. Umberleigh-Smith, but it was not for some time that it dawned on me that he had invited her to my flat that night. "You see," he said, "one thing I know about detection is that wherever possible you get together as many suspects as you can at the actual place of the crime."

"You mean you know one thing about detective *fiction?*" I suggested coldly.

"You get them all together," he elaborated, not permitting my sarcasm to discourage him, "in the actual place, and then you spring your surprise."

"Dear me," I said, "so we're going to have a surprise too?"

"That's right," said Mandrake, getting to his feet again. "I asked you yesterday if there was some sort of screen in the flat, but I can see you haven't found one. Those two tall bookcases will do if you'll give me a hand."

He was tugging one of them away from the wall, and rather

than let him spill Cyprian's first editions all over the room, I helped him, if only to keep it upright, till he had it and its fellow arranged to his liking under the mask of Cyprian, that was due to stand in the foyer of the Aldwych Theatre just so soon as we could remember to deliver it or the Aldwych could concern itself to collect it. They now cut off a corner of the room, leaving a gap at one side.

"And now," I said, "suppose you explain what it's all about."

"But I told you. It's coming to a head, here, tonight."

"What is?"

"The meeting of all the people who made those records."

"Don't talk nonsense. You surely don't imagine they'll come?"

"They're on their way."

"Good God, man, are you serious?"

"I've always been serious about this murder. It's you who want to drop the whole thing just as it's getting interesting."

"You've had the damned impertinence to invite a whole lot of women to my flat without consulting me?"

"I tried my hardest to consult you yesterday evening. You kept slipping through my fingers in and out of the bathroom, so that I couldn't even get started. I simply had to make my plans, taking it for granted that you'd co-operate. If you won't" —he swung round and loomed over me, while his eyes bored into me with disconcerting penetration—"I can only assume that you have very good reasons for not wanting to find out who murdered your uncle."

I tried not to flinch under his gaze. "It isn't that," I said, feeling it unjust that a manner so deceptively mild and school-boyish should conceal such inflexible granite. "It's just that I don't think it's a very good idea and I don't think it will come off. The women who made those records would be far too scared to come."

But Mandrake thought they'd come.

"What have you told them?"

"Oh, different things to each woman. Naturally I had to

162

vary my technique with each. I told Mrs. Creel, who made the suicide record, and Janet Drury, the actress, that Cyprian had left them a little remembrance in his will which would arrive by messenger within a day or so. In both cases they were scared that the messenger would come when they weren't alone and would have to be explained. I then suggested that if they cared to drop in for it this evening I should be alone at the flat, putting a few last things in order."

"And whom did they suppose you to be?"

"Professor Mandrake, of course. I'm afraid they also understood that I was an executor to Cyprian's will."

"There must be penalties for that sort of misrepresentation."

"I expect there are. Do you suppose any of them will expose me, even if they suspect my imposture?"

"Possibly not. What do you propose to give them?"

"Well, finally, that's rather up to you. After all, Cyprian left you his personal effects. While you were out yesterday I did have the forethought to wrap up one of his cigarette boxes for Mrs. Creel, and I felt sure the little actress would appreciate his lilac-silk dressing gown."

"You seem to have attended to everything. What did you do about Miss Pritchard?"

"I was obliged to wire her. I put, 'Record compromising you among Uncle's effects. Advise you collect personally, nine-fifteen tomorrow Sunday, avoid undesirable publicity.' I'm afraid I had to sign your name."

"But the record Miss Pritchard made isn't in existence."

"No, but I soaked off the label of a rather scratched Deanna Durbin I happened to have at home and made it into a secure parcel. She's unlikely to want to undo it while she's here and she certainly won't want to play it."

The whole thing sounded like a crazy and amateur bungle. I felt furious with Mandrake for arranging it without my knowledge, but after all, I thought, in the absence of Marcia it could only prove ineffectual. And if it needed a complete fiasco to quench Mandrake's alarming zeal, let us have it and get it over.

"And if nothing happens," I said quite cheerfully, "we're going to be left with a hell of a lot to explain."

"We'll think of something," said Mandrake. "They're all in too vulnerable a position to make serious trouble. For the rest, you'll gather Myrtle Best didn't require any special technique. Mrs. Umberleigh-Smith wasn't very much trouble either, once I'd found out where she lived and got inside the house. I simply told her she'd been mentioned in a client's will —someone who'd known her in what I ventured to describe rather meaningly as *the old days*, and would she prefer to come along by herself and collect it, or receive the legacy by messenger along with a communication outlining the circumstances which had aroused my client's gratitude? She jumped to it in a second and promised to be right here on the dot. She even showed me out herself, by the back way. A very reasonable woman. The sixth . . ."

"There were only five records. You know that."

"So you told me," agreed Mandrake, "but I have always been convinced that there were six. I have long ago abandoned the theory that I had your entire confidence, and so when it came to the point, I didn't give you mine, and I issued a sixth invitation just in case."

"She won't come."

"Who won't come?"

His eyes were watching me, hard and humourless as a cat's. I felt my scalp prickle. What a fool I had been to consider him a bungling amateur. I was the bungler. I didn't answer, trying to think how I could prevent Marcia from coming.

"I admit I had to make use of a little subtlety," said Mandrake, "but I assure you all my invitations were accepted."

I put out my hand for the telephone, but a sudden sharpening of his features warned me that this was what he intended. Suppose he were bluffing, that he knew only that there had been six voices, but didn't actually suspect Marcia? Suppose he hadn't invited her at all, but had invented the whole scheme to get me to disclose my sixth suspect—could I telephone her without revealing her identity? Of course not. The flats had their own internal switchboard. You called the operator and asked for your number. Mandrake would remember the number and check it later. His face fell as I drew back my hand.

"If you feel I've gone too far," he suggested with unlikely deference, "you could telephone and put her off."

I said, "Yes, to be sure, I could, if I had the slightest idea who your sixth suspect is."

"Haven't you?" said Mandrake. "Then why were you so sure she wouldn't come?" We were playing the game cautiously, step by step, both determined to give away nothing.

"I don't think anyone will come," I answered. "But if they do, I feel sure you'll entertain them admirably. On the other hand, I'm going to the post. There's no reason why you shouldn't come with me if you feel like it."

I stood in the doorway, challenging him. For it occurred to me that if he agreed to accompany me, I should know that the whole thing had been a bluff, to try and find out my sixth suspect, and that he hadn't invited anyone. He watched me distrustfully, looked at his watch, and then before he could make a definite move one way or the other, the door buzzer went. I got to the door before him. If it were Marcia, I could head her off, but it wasn't. I instantly recognized the mayoress-elect of Hooper's Cross. Fair enough. Mandrake *had* issued his invitations, and Mrs. Umberleigh-Smith's arrival would necessitate his remaining in the flat. I muttered a swift good-bye to Mandrake and dived past his visitor on the threshold. Whatever he did with her, it would give me time to get round to Marcia and warn her.

Marcia opened the door to me. She looked tired and rather white. She put out her hand and gave a bleak little cry of "Simon," then she drew back and waited for me to speak.

"Hold everything," I said, and pushed past her and closed the door. Then I spoke quickly. "I don't know what story Mandrake's told you," I said, "but you're not to come, and if he telephones or tries to speak to you, you'd better not say I've been here. I can't stop now. Do you understand?"

"Not in the least," said Marcia. "Mandrake hasn't said anything or asked me to go anywhere."

"He hasn't? He hasn't asked you to come to my flat this evening?"

"No."

"Then it *was* a bluff. Forget that I came round at all, will you?"

She was as tense as I was. She said, rather shakily, "Don't go. Please. Mandrake's in it now, isn't he? I can't just be left, not knowing what anyone is thinking. Please."

I said, "Mandrake arrived at my flat with a plan to get all his suspects together there this evening and startle one of them into some sort of confession. I'd told him there were only five records, to try and keep you out of it, but he said he was sure there'd been six and he'd invited six women. He wouldn't tell me who the sixth was, and now I realise it was a bluff to try and startle me into saying who it was. But in case he knew, and really had arranged for you to be there, I had to warn you."

She stood for a moment trying to get what I was telling her into focus, then she said, "Did you say they were coming to your flat this evening, the six people Mandrake suspects?"

"That's what he said, but it's clear there'll be only five."

"Why? Why should there be only five? Perhaps he suspects someone else altogether. What time were they to come?"

"Now. The first one's arrived already."

A queer light of battle flickered in Marcia's eyes. "I'm going to be there."

"Over my dead body."

"I've got to be there. I've got to know what goes on. Why shouldn't I just walk in to see you?"

"Because Mandrake thinks I'm here now. He'd have followed me if one of his suspects hadn't turned up."

"How do you know he thinks you're here? You didn't tell him?"

"I said I had to post a letter."

"Being an American, you didn't have to know the last post on Sunday goes at half-past four. Did either of you mention my name?"

"No."

"Then I've got to know if it really is me or someone else he suspects. I shall go round right away and ask for you. When he says you're out, I'll wait. You saunter in a little later, having posted your letter. All right?"

"All right, if you say so, but I don't like it."

"Considering how little you like the whole thing—it was nice of you to come." Her fingers found mine and pressed them. "Give me ten minutes," she said, "before you get back from the post. When you see me, be surprised, but don't overdo it."

When I returned to the flat there was no need to look surprised or otherwise. My latchkey made no sound, and as I let myself into the tiny lobby, no light was burning. I thought at first the flat was deserted. Then, through the study door, I heard Mandrake's voice. I opened the door and found the study almost in darkness, with various shadowy shapes around the room, and at the end, near the bookcases, Mandrake's vast bulk on his feet and talking.

"Now, ladies," he was saying, and even his voice loomed larger than life empowered by his own fantastic enthusiasm for this extraordinary make-believe, "I shall explain why you have each been summoned in this way to this place." A confused murmur broke out from the women, but he went on urbanely. "As each one of you has some reason not to wish to make herself or her presence here known, I do not propose to introduce you to one another. Your anonymity will be preserved so long as not one of you does anything herself to destroy it. For this reason I asked you each to wait in separate rooms and did not call you together until I had plunged this room into darkness. Mr. Crane and I have certain instructions from his uncle, the late Cyprian Druse. It is our wish to carry these out while causing as little pain or embarrassment as possible. You will best assist us by being seated and remaining silent."

He placed his hands on the shoulders of the largest shadow present, whom I assumed to be Mrs. Umberleigh-Smith, and pressed her into a chair.

"That's right," he said, moving round the room, arranging

the other shapes in chairs, "be seated and relax your apprehension. There is nothing whatever to fear. Even if anyone
should recognise any other, each has sufficient reason not to
wish to disclose that other's presence, for by so doing she would
disclose her own. Cyprian planned this meeting partly from a
genuine desire to restore to the women he had at any time
loved certain pieces of property which he felt it would console
them to have, and partly from another motive which I shall
presently disclose. If you all do as I suggest, the letter of his
wishes may be performed without causing anyone embarrassment."

"It won't cause me any embarrassment," said Myrtle Best's
voice. "Cyprian and I were, naturally, the best of friends and
I was deeply bereaved at his death, but I don't mind in the
least who knows that he remembered me in his will and I've
certainly nothing to hide."

"Nor have I," said Miss Pritchard's quick, nervous voice.
"I came here merely on business at my agent's request. I shall
be glad to be allowed to complete my business and depart. I've
a long way to go."

"Yet it was worth the journey," said Mandrake, "or you
wouldn't have come."

"Ai-ve simply no ideah what it's all abeout," stated the
torturedly refined voice of Mrs. Umberleigh-Smith. "The
wheole thing is a scandalous imposition . . ."

"There is no scandal—*yet*," said Mandrake, moving shad-
owily back from the group, "and I shall endeavour to handle
events so that there is no need for scandal. Apart from the
trifling sentimental objects which Cyprian wished to bequeath
to you ladies, and apart from all properties mentioned in his
will, Cyprian possessed certain other property of a definite
financial value whose existence was not disclosed even to Mr.
Chiddingstone, his solicitor, who is also my co-executor for
the will. Such possessions, if disclosed, would by law be put
towards the payment of his debts, for my friend, as you are
doubtless aware, died in debt. I, however, am putting friendship before the law. It was Cyprian's intention that this prop-

168

erty should go to the woman, if there is such a woman, who had genuinely loved him, although he has always claimed to doubt the existence of genuine love. On this question he had a great deal to say, and tonight, if the things he believed in prove true, he will have more . . ."

He held the pause till the breathing of one of the women in the room grew fast and a little hysterical, then his voice quickened and dropped an octave and became charged with sinister import. "Though he never disclosed the fact to anyone but myself, Cyprian made various experiments in what I will term the occult, and produced some startling results. He believed that a man's presence remained for some time after his death near the things and places he had loved when alive, and might, in favourable conditions, communicate either by sight or sound with those who are receptive. He assured me that when his wishes had been carried out, as they have been tonight, he himself would disclose his intentions as to the disposal of his property, after he had spoken of the nature of love, and ascertained, as he was sure he would ascertain, if there were any love for him in any heart in this room. *That moment is now.* I charge you all to secrecy. What may come or may not come is not of my seeking. I have fulfilled my promise and carried out my debt to the dead."

Mandrake's voice had sunk to a whisper which mustered the shadows in the room and gave them a terrible reality. "Cyprian Druse," he said distinctly, as though calling on the man to answer, and as he did so, the mask of Cyprian over the bookcase began faintly to glow in a horrid greenish light. A gasp went through the room, almost a moan. In the following silence the unmistakable voice of my uncle began to speak.

"The human race," said Cyprian's voice, in easy, conversational tones, "is inspired or tormented by a thousand different emotions, urges or reactions, all of which are lumped together by popular usage under the main heading of love. All of them are, admittedly, in a sense, expressions of love, but love of self only; in other words, greed or a desire to perpetuate. If I could find, out of my whole life's experience, one example of genuine, selfless love, how happy I should live, how happily indeed I should die . . ."

Someone was on her feet and brushing past me to the door. "A couple of grown men playing a silly practical joke," cried Marcia's voice, tense and furious. "Why, that's a recorded session of the National Quiz. Cyprian hadn't any undisclosed property and he never dabbled in the occult. I suppose you hoped one of us would faint or scream or do something."

Light flooded the room. Marcia stood at the door with her hand on the switch. I saw her eyes go from one to another of the greensick women round the table: Mrs. Creel, Mrs. Umberleigh-Smith, Myrtle Best, Janet Drury and Miss Pritchard. Mumbling angrily, Mandrake came out from behind the bookcases, where Cyprian's expensive gramophone was still playing the record he must have obtained from the B.B.C. No one was looking at Marcia when she gasped and put out her hand and pitched forward in a dead faint.

CHAPTER SEVENTEEN

I lifted Marcia from the doorway and laid her on the couch, while the other women made their departure more or less hurriedly and with more or less dignity. Only Mrs. Best stuck out for a legacy and only Miss Pritchard insisted on taking her record. For the rest, they were glad to be out of the place on any terms and each grateful that it had been Marcia rather than herself whose collapse had relieved the tension.

I crouched over Marcia, loathing Mandrake for his horrible theatrical trick which had, nonetheless, found a vulnerable spot in the strongest set of nerves in the room. She was not long coming to. As she opened her eyes the record was speaking again in Cyprian's voice, "in fact it is the theme of my just completed volume, *Analysis of a Woman 'in Love,'* that if a woman cannot find an object for this overpowering passion to squander herself, she will invent one which doesn't exist and squander herself upon that . . ."

"Turn it off," said Marcia in a mutter that came through clenched teeth. "You've got what you wanted, haven't you? Turn that horrible thing off."

Mandrake went behind the bookcases and took off the record. "There's no necessity to be so vehement," he said, "nor so resentful. After all, *you* weren't even invited. You came of your own accord."

Marcia settled herself more firmly on the couch and met his eyes levelly. "But you have to admit that you wanted me to come even if you didn't precisely ask me. And you have to admit it wouldn't have been nearly such a success without me."

"That's true."

"Then I *was* the sixth suspect that you had in mind, wasn't I? And you did try and bluff poor Simon here into revealing that I was his suspect too?"

Mandrake's vanity was stung by her voice. "Yes," he answered, "and I should have succeeded if that confounded woman hadn't arrived just when she did."

"Oh, but you have succeeded." Marcia's voice was taut and vibrant, as though a metal cat could purr. "You mustn't underestimate your achievement. Simon did suspect me, while I'm sure I was always your favourite, and here I am in a dead faint at the sound of my victim's voice. What more could you want?"

Mandrake spoke slowly. "I don't want any more."

Marcia said, "Can I have a cigarette? They always give them a cigarette, you know."

I gave her a cigarette and lit it. My hand was shaking but hers was perfectly still. She took a long pull and looked coolly into Mandrake's eyes. "What are you going to do?" she asked.

Mandrake answered very quietly, "What do you suppose?"

Marcia smiled. "You'll look an awful fool if you hand me

over to the law," she said. "I've got an alibi like the Bank of England. From two o'clock till five on the day Cyprian died I was having a permanent wave. I can produce any sort of evidence you like to prove it, from the appointment book to the hairdresser and a couple of assistants."

Stronger than relief or any other emotion, I felt a surging anger with Marcia for never having told me. For letting me suffer and torment myself so long when she could have put me out of my misery so easily at any time. I stood up stiffly, finding I had been crouching on the floor beside her till my muscles were cramped, and half bowed to her.

"The thing I find so fascinating about the English is their wonderful sense of humour," I said bitterly. "It was kind of you to look in. I hardly think we need detain you any further."

She got to her feet. "Thanks for a wonderful evening," she said, catching my tone. "I won't ask you to take my word about it, naturally. The shop is Alberto in Berkeley Street. You'll find them in the book." Then she was at the door and then she was gone.

"Now isn't that just fine?" I said, hating Mandrake for a bungler and myself for a fool, and hating Marcia for having so cruelly made me a fool. But Mandrake's detachment had reasserted itself. "I'll check her alibi tomorrow," he said. "I'm giving a lecture at ten, but I daresay there'll be someone in the shop who can look up the appointment book before then. In any case, it isn't important. It wouldn't be worth her while inventing an alibi that wouldn't hold when she knows I shall check it immediately. We can be pretty certain she didn't do it. She wouldn't have come if she'd done it, nor would any of them. Did you ever see such a bunch of lily-livered ineffectuals?"

"Then what in the world was the purpose in throwing the party?"

"I thought we might stumble on something." His eyes narrowed. "And we have, in a roundabout fashion. We've had our money on the wrong horse. Because an attempt had been made to break into that cabinet at the same time as the murder was done, we've both been certain that the motive for the murder was inside that cabinet. But why? Couldn't it equally well have been something that was *thought* to be inside the cabinet? After all, that *isn't* a record cabinet, although it contained records. It's a perfectly ordinary filing cabinet. Why shouldn't the murderer have been looking for papers of some sort, and merely tried to pick that lock because it was the most likely thing in the room to contain them? You said yourself there were no papers elsewhere in the room. What happened to Cyprian's manuscripts?"

"He never kept them. He destroyed all drafts as soon as they were delivered to the newspapers."

"But the manuscripts of his books, what happened to them?"

"The last one had gone to be typed a little before his death, Brady told me."

"Would that be the one he was holding forth about in that last quiz programme? *Analysis of a Woman 'in Love'*? Do you suppose there was anything in that which was going to do harm to somebody?"

"It would be very unlike my uncle if there weren't."

Mandrake's gaze had turned inwards again. "We all know he never had a creative idea of his own in his life. Is it likely that the woman whose love he decided to analyse in that volume was an imaginary woman? Isn't it more in keeping with his character to have taken a real woman, whose love for him or for someone else had been indiscreetly revealed to him, and made her the guinea pig for a cruel investigation? Suppose that was the case—suppose his victim knew or suspected, and, listening in to that session, realised that he was going to make his findings about her public . . ." Mandrake thumped his palm with his fist. "I'd like to see that manuscript. Where is it?"

"It's with Miss Tangent."

"Damn this lecture tomorrow," he said. "I'll have to ask you to do this for me. Find Miss Tangent in the telephone book, go along and pay for the manuscript and collect it on the strength of your relationship with Cyprian. Skim it, and if there seems to be anything in it that requires consideration, telephone me.

173

I'll be at the Cadogan Institute from ten o'clock. So long as I'm not actually in the middle of the lecture, I can talk to you." He was on his feet at last. "Will you do it?" he asked.

"All right," I said.

He left me alone in the emptiness and loneliness of the sadly disordered flat. I went to the bathroom and there in the tooth glass was Hazel's orchid still flourishing, for orchids, unlike mignonette, stand up to almost anything and come through the most disillusioning experiences unmarked.

In the morning I looked up Miss Tangent's address in the telephone book and found it was in Wanstead, which Brady told me meant a journey through the most outlandish part of London. I set out without enthusiasm and met Marcia, almost on my threshold. I said "Good morning" shortly and didn't stop.

She said, "You seem to be in a tremendous hurry."

"I have to get to Wanstead Flats."

"Must you really? A bittern couldn't be building there, by any chance?"

"I'm going to collect Cyprian's manuscript from the typist."

"I suppose in the parts you come from they've never heard of a newfangled institution called the G.P.O.? Or don't you trust it?"

"Mandrake thinks it may contain the real reason that my uncle met his end."

"Do you always have to do exactly as Mandrake tells you?"

"I promised I would. In any case, I'd like to see the manuscript. Cyprian's publications didn't usually spread much happiness. I'd prefer to see this one before it goes any further."

"Why not ring up and ask for it, or write?"

"I think I'd rather go."

"Just as you please. It's the end of the world. Shall I come with you?"

"To the end of the world?"

"Well, to Wanstead Flats anyway."

"If you've nothing better to do."

It seemed profitless to wonder why Marcia should decide to come with me to what she regarded as the end of the world, but I refused to suppose she was doing it for the charm of my society. Mandrake had accepted her alibi and, subject to its validity, had dismissed her from his mind, while I could not forget her inconsistencies and the earring, nor that she had insisted on being at his sinister party and had been in such a state of tension that she had fainted at the sound of Cyprian's voice. Marcia had her alibi, no doubt, but she also had her own reasons for wanting to know everything we knew—including what I should find at Miss Tangent's office—and they were hardly likely to be the reasons she would offer to me if I asked.

Towards the end of the interminable journey she said, "Whatever makes Mandrake think the manuscript could have anything to do with Cyprian's death?"

I said, "None of those women killed him. None of them had the cold courage to come back if they'd done a murder, even to remove some clue that connected them with it. You had the courage, but you didn't kill him either. The person who killed him and picked that lock did it for something they believed to be in the cabinet but that wasn't. Not a record; there's no reason why they should have known it contained records at all. They could have been looking for something else, couldn't they?"

"Why do you ask me? I thought you'd decided I didn't do it."

"If I have, it's no fault of yours. You could have convinced me you didn't do it at any time if you'd made the faintest attempt. You never did. You *wanted* me to think it might be you."

"Did I?"

"At first I thought you'd done it. Then I was sure you hadn't, that it was just your damnable insolence that refused to clear yourself of something I'd no right to suspect. But at Barrow Lock you changed quite suddenly after breakfast. You went out of your way to bewitch me, to blind me to every consideration but your loveliness and desirability. But you still wouldn't lift a finger to assure me you were innocent—not even after you'd found the earring in your shoe. So I think it wasn't fear for your skin that prompted your sudden affection. Was it?"

She looked out of the trolley-bus window. "Did no further possibility present itself?"

"The possibility that you were genuinely attracted to me?" I said harshly. "Yes, it presented itself. A man who sees an oasis in the desert is bound to feel some sort of emotion, even if he's got a map and knows the oasis isn't there."

"Sometimes the people who make maps haven't all the facts at hand. . . ."

"You want me to believe you fell in love with me between going upstairs to look for the darning silk and coming downstairs without it?"

She looked abashed and unhappy. "No, I don't. I don't want you to believe anything about me. I think this is where we get out."

When I had found Miss Tangent's office I explained who I was and asked if Cyprian's work was completed. Miss Tangent looked surprised. The manuscript had been paid for and taken away earlier that very morning by the publisher's representative. I thanked her and withdrew, then on an impulse went into a telephone box and dialled the Corncrake Press, Cyprian's publishers. No one there had heard any word of the arrival of the manuscript, nor had any messenger been sent to collect it.

When I told Marcia, outside the call box, she said, "Corncrake's are a biggish firm. They mightn't necessarily know."

"I think they'd know. They'd never heard of Miss Tangent, and were wondering when the manuscript would arrive."

"Well, there it is. There's nothing you can do. Perhaps it's been sent to the flat in the usual way."

I didn't answer but went back to Miss Tangent's office and explained what the publishers had told me. I asked who had interviewed the messenger. It appeared that she had spoken to the typist who had carried out the work, a Miss Massey. Miss Massey was sent for.

I asked Miss Massey what had happened to the original script from which she had made her copies and she told me that the messenger had particularly asked for it as well. "Actually I hadn't finished the last couple of chapters, but the lady said it was needed urgently and took it and paid in full."

I said, "What was the nature of the manuscript? Was it a work of research or imagination?" The girl gazed at me through her glasses. "Was it fact or fiction; about things or people; was it interesting? Did you want to know what happened at the end?"

"Well, it was interesting, really, the way it began, first the man's letter then the woman's, then another from the man and so on, but then it kept breaking off and going on *about* the letters, what must have been in their minds and that, when you wanted to find out what had happened to the people."

"And did you?"

"I don't know. The lady fetched it away before I'd got to the end."

"Who were the people? Who were the letters addressed to?"

"The man's weren't addressed properly at all; they began 'My Dear,' and they were carbon copies of typewriting, not signed at all. The woman's were handwritten in violet ink. They began 'Colin,' and they were just signed with a letter M."

I saw Marcia's knuckles whiten against the horrible little metal office chair.

I said, "What was the woman like who collected the manuscript?"

"Oh, medium height, I should say, not tall, middle-aged, greyish hair, wearing a dark suit."

"Had you ever seen her before?"

"Not to remember."

"Was nothing familiar about her—her manner—her voice?"

"Well, now that you ask me, her voice did put me in mind of that one on the National Quiz, that Mrs. Grey. But it's hard to say unless you've seen their faces."

I thanked the girl and we went. Outside I said, "When did you know who it was?"

"I *don't* know."

"Letters in violet ink addressed to Colin?"

"I've never heard of Colin."

"Mabel Grey used to write to him sitting at a café table in a station waiting room. Mandrake told me."

"There are dozens of men called Colin."

"Dozens of women use violet ink—grey-haired, inconspicuous little women whose voices just might be familiar to girls like Miss Massey."

"Oh God, if she had to fall in love, why must she let the letters get into the hands of your uncle of all people?"

"Why did she wait till now to get them back?"

"She can't have known where they were until you told her the typist's name last Saturday, and Saturday they would be closed. This morning must have been her first chance."

"Then why must she go herself and risk being recognised?"

Marcia looked deathly sick. "I'm afraid I know the answer to that. Once she had got the manuscript, it didn't matter any more."

"Didn't matter?"

"I don't suppose she meant to—hang around. Don't you remember she kept saying she'd got so little time to finish her housing scheme."

"Yes, but——"

"I've remembered something else. On Friday when I arrived she said there was a wasp's nest in the garden and she wondered if it was still as easy to get cyanide as it had been in my schooldays when Stephen used it to take their nests for my protection." Her eyes dilated with horror. "*Cyanide*—it went clear over my head."

"We've got to do something," I said, but she was whimpering now like a child.

"What can we do? We're miles away, right the other side of London, and we don't even know where she'll go."

"She won't try and do away with herself till she's destroyed the manuscript. The chances are a hundred to one she'll go quietly home and make a thorough job of burning it before she thinks about anything else. Besides, I don't suppose it's nearly as easy to get cyanide now as it was when you were a child."

"She'll get something."

CHAPTER EIGHTEEN

There was no hope of a taxi, and after ten minutes we gave up the attempt and set out once more on the interminable journey on foot, by trolley-bus and finally by train, growing dusty, hungry and horribly apprehensive towards the last. Once I said, "If only you'd told me at the start, right at the beginning, I shouldn't have let you down. I'd have tried to help you."

"Right at the start I didn't even know myself. When Cyprian died I wanted to get my record back. It compromised me a little, at any rate made a fool of me, but I never regarded it as more important than that because I didn't suppose Cyprian had been murdered. That paragraph in the paper told me your name, and as you never seemed to go out, I rang you up and asked you to meet me. I looked for the record and failed, and that was that. When you came and accused me, I didn't even trouble to defend myself. I thought the whole thing was a piece of audacity on your part and I was furious with you for having heard the record."

"Even though I gave it back to you?"

"Yes. Chivalry in the circumstances wasn't enough. I wanted never to have made the thing. Since you *had* heard it —had heard me, with all guards down, making a spectacular fool of myself, the least you could do, short of dropping down dead, was to arrange that I never set eyes on you again, but you had to turn up at Barrow Lock. Either you'd come because you still suspected me of this fantastic murder or because you claimed to be in love with me."

"In either case, it couldn't matter less?"

She turned to me almost with apology. "How could I take you seriously? I didn't even take your murder story seriously until I found the other earring in Mabel's workbox. I walked downstairs in a daze and went into the outhouse where they kept the salvage. Last week's *New Statesman* had a bit torn out of the corner of the 'This England' page. The world turned upside down. It was like waking into a nightmare. If Cyprian could have been murdered and if Mabel could have done it, it was equally possible that you had come to Barrow Lock to find out about her instead of me. She had asked you back to lunch and might give away anything. I must prevent that. I followed you, and when I asked you why you'd come, you said, 'I thought it was time your aunt Mabel and I got together.'"

"I don't even remember saying it. It didn't mean anything. I came because of you."

"I couldn't know that."

"So you arranged to meet me and to dine with me in London. You even endured my clumsy embraces to make absolutely certain I should be on the London train that evening."

"You can't always choose your weapons. I only thanked heaven they were adequate for what I had to do."

"More than adequate, dear heart. You overplayed your hand appallingly. Red sequins, too. It couldn't be that you overestimated my intelligence?"

She blushed. "No, it couldn't be that, could it? I suppose I based my characterisation on the assumption that I had to appeal to the type that would fall in love with the first murderess he thought he'd met."

"Reasonable enough; but it would have been even more reasonable and infinitely less painful if you'd told me the truth."

"How could I know? Look, Simon, supposing, through some combination of circumstances, I had killed Cyprian, I think, when I realised what you felt and what you were like, I should have told you the truth and taken my chance. But to the best of my knowledge you didn't fall in love with Mabel. You might have taken a totally different attitude once you suspected *her*. I couldn't know, could I?"

"But why did you need to torture me by making me think you were guilty? Why did you need to humiliate us both by pretending to be fond of me? We both deserved better than that."

"So long as you suspected me you weren't likely to follow up any suspicion you might have of her. So long as you were in love with *me* you wouldn't turn me over to the law. Presently you would go back and the whole episode would become for you an outlandish, rather highly coloured wild oat, quite detached from real life. Besides, I had to keep the whole thing a little out of drawing. It's hard to explain, but you see, the nicer you were and the more I could see I was hurting you, the more I had to keep a grip on myself for fear I should give in and tell you the truth. I had to keep telling myself I was playing a part."

"I see. I'm trying to see."

"After I'd planted the earring in my shoe I thought I was out of the wood, but when you told me about Mandrake's horrible party, and said he'd invited six suspects, and I knew I wasn't one of them, I had to be there, to find out who the sixth was. It was dark when he opened the door. I'd no way of knowing whether Mabel was there or not. When he started the record of Cyprian's voice, at first, I didn't recognise it. When I did, and I knew that Mabel would be speaking soon, I realised that somewhere in that recording there might be something that would startle her into giving herself away. I took a chance and switched on the lights. Mabel wasn't there. I suppose the relief was too much for me. She was safe. Neither of you could ever have suspected her at all, so it was safe to tell you my alibi and be done with the whole thing. Even to save her I should never have gone through with a trial, and if you didn't suspect her then, there didn't seem any risk that you ever would." Marcia looked wearily out of the window, seeing nothing. "And yet it was that recording that gave you the clue in the end, so perhaps Mandrake wasn't such a bungler after all."

She broke off and her face was naked, with all pretences gone and all barriers down. She looked strained and desperately tired. "It hasn't been any sort of fun for me these last few days." I thought she was going to cry, there in the carriage full of strangers, but she set her jaw and breathed a couple of gulps of air. "And now," she said dully, "I wonder what's waiting for us to tackle next."

We got a car for the final stage of our journey and arrived at Cedar Lodge at last. The front door was open but there was no sign of anyone inside. Mabel's study was in disorder, with charred papers in the grate, and on top of the ashes, a fresh batch, just beginning to burn. I snatched them from the fireplace and pressed out the flames. The first page was dated with that day's date and began with the one word "Colin."

"It's a letter," said Marcia. "Perhaps you ought to see what it says. I'll go on looking for her—or Stephen or someone."

I picked up the sheaf of papers and began to read their extraordinary content.

"Colin," she had written, "I don't know why I am writing this to you. Is it habit or must we assume that the 'balance of my mind is disturbed,' or is it a desperate attempt to justify myself—to myself? For it is more and more borne upon me that we neither have nor can have any positive proof of the existence of anyone but ourselves, since between one human being and another there is no communication, no sharing of anything felt; and while we are telling one thing, they who listen are hearing another.

"But for a little while I was not alone; for a little while I thought you heard me; and every small thing happening became an adventure that I should presently tell you in a letter. The colours of every day became brighter, like colours after rain, because there was someone to show them to; because there was you.

"Even your first letter of all, which was sent on from the B.B.C., along with half a dozen others, was quite different from anything else. The others were from people who wanted me to meet them or help a cause for them or buy something or open a bazaar or advise them about their lives. You wanted nothing of me; you seemed already to stand side by side with me, knowing all that needed to be known, and already I seemed to know all I had to know about you. You never asked to meet me and I never wanted to meet you, but because of you I was complete. You knew what I was fighting for. You alone understood what I stood for in my perpetual battle of wits with Cyprian Druse. I used to feel that he was evil, was the canker at the heart of all things; and I used to fear that he was, perhaps, reality, and that pitting my puny wit and strength against him was like a pygmy beating the face of a giant; but I had to go on. Your first letter came after one such battle; a battle I seemed to have lost and which he, with characteristic brilliance, had certainly won. You wrote and thanked me and told me you were with me. Then I knew that nothing I did was wasted. I knew that you were listening; that I spoke for some-one beside myself. After that I was never alone. Even when I lost I was never alone. When I was ill or in the dark or mortally afraid I was never alone. You were with me.

"And throughout the day anything that I had to do that was hurtful or distasteful was made bearable by the consciousness that you were in the world. Because I think that for women like me, loneliness is the occupational disease; loneliness of the heart or the spirit—I was too little alone in the flesh. And I think it is of loneliness that many people die, and that presently I must die, dear heart, oh, my dear; while the balance of my mind is disturbed, or perhaps while for the briefest moment that balance is restored.

"When you wrote that you had come to love me and I faced the fact that without you life would have no meaning, I was content. I knew that you, too, were tied. There was no question of any meeting or contact between us. Nor any need. We were complete, you and I. Nothing that passed between us falsified our commitments to the others. In fact I, at least, became gentler and more able to be patient with factors of my life which had previously seemed intolerable—now that I perceived some pattern in existence, some basic sanity on which I could depend. There was no suffering I could not have endured, borne up by this. If you had died, I could have faced even that with the courage you would have demanded of me. But you didn't die.

"When your letters stopped, at first I went on writing, care of the tobacconist in Privet Street. If something were wrong you would need my assurance doubly, and even though you were unable for some reason to send any word to me, I could not bear to feel that you might send to the address for my letters and find nothing. But there was deadly fear in my heart. Illness was something we hadn't visualised or planned against. I had no picture of your private circumstances. You had not said you were married, only 'tied.' You had not said if you were rich or poor. You might be ill, in need of care, in need of money and I shouldn't know. And if you died, no one would tell me. I racked my brain and at last I decided to go to the accommodation address and make them tell me where you lived. Then I would go to your house and ask for the householder and pretend I was taking some sort of survey of public opinion which necessitated my finding the number of adults living in the house and asking a few routine questions. I knew I could learn something that way. People do not readily close doors in my face.

"I dressed with curious care. I even wore the little crystal wings that you had sent me—for the first time—since I never wear things like that. The papers, which no one had looked at, were in the hall. I picked up the *New Statesman* to read in the train, though I never really looked at it. I took a taxi to the Park and then went on foot to find Privet Street. The tobacconist told me the address without much difficulty. 'The gentleman' had paid him a monthly sum to readdress the letters to him at Flat 612, Pendervil Mansions.

"When I found myself on the threshold of a luxurious block of flats I realised that you could hardly be in need of care or attention, but it never occurred to me that you would not be in need of me. I avoided the porters and went up the stairs to the sixth floor and then followed arrows to 612 along the carpeted passages. I rang the bell and waited, rehearsing my opening sentences. I think the servant was out, for after a longish time the door was opened by Cyprian Druse.

"Everything I had planned to say vanished and I stood, on the brink of nightmare, stupidly saying your name.

"He said, 'Yes, I am Colin Cheverel,' and then my brain reeled and my blood turned to water and the carpet began to rise to greet me. He put out his hand and took me by the arm and said, 'I see the game is up. You'd better come inside.'

"He steadied me over the threshold into the room and put me on a settee, where I sat, growing old and cold with horror, while my brain very gradually accepted the fact that I was terribly, horribly, sickly and hideously *funny;* that my heart was pickled and exposed in a bottle of faintly green liquid and my body naked and accursed and ashamed.

"He offered me a cigarette but I didn't put out my hand to take it, and he put the case on his desk. I suppose he was nervous at what he had done, for his hand shook a little. He said, 'Thank you for your letters, Mabel. You have given me a great deal of pleasure.'

"That shrivelled-souled popinjay was thanking me for the letters I had written to you!

"Only then, through the ice that was forming inch thick over my heart, did I register the fact that *you* were nowhere in the world and never had been. That you had only ever existed in my imagination. That I was alone for all time with reality; and reality was Cyprian Druse.

"Everything in the room is etched in my mind, as I sat there not hearing any of the pretence he made at conversation: the soft, beautiful carpets, the thick amber wallpaper, the exquisite pictures, the busts and portraits of Cyprian, the tooled leather backs of books in their open shelves; the moulded ceiling and the high, huge-paned windows, through which I could hear the magically distant hum of London.

"I wanted to die; to be dead; never to have lived; but his voice went on talking and presently I began to think again. What he had said was true: women loved because they had to, for no reason in the beloved, only for their own need to love. A woman, he had said, would love though the object be loathsome, so long as no better was to hand; and if there were no object, she would invent one. He had proved it and I was the guinea pig. Sharp and high, across whatever he was saying, I heard my own voice say, 'I must have my letters,' and he smiled.

"If the devils smile in hell, as I do not doubt, they must look as Cyprian Druse looked then. He began to tell me that it had been my privilege to take part with him in a most profound experiment and that it would be in the interests of humanity to place his findings before the world in his forthcoming volume, *Analysis of a Woman 'in Love.'* He assured me that naturally the name of his human guinea pig would not be disclosed to the public. But I knew very well that the letters spoke for themselves. They were unmistakably mine and, printed in the context he outlined, they made nonsense of everything I had believed and was fighting for, and of everything I had helped other people to believe. He knew it too.

"I came down to pleading with him, but I might as well have pleaded with his bust. He was revelling in the situation, extracting the last ounce of sensation from placing me at last in a position from which there was no escape except in total humiliation. He called me to the window and, with an expression of seeming kindliness, asked me to consider the infinite littleness of the antlike human beings crawling on the pavement so far below. He assured me that, in the interests of science and research into human motives—which he would have me suppose were his sole motives behind the whole affair—I was no more important than any of those, and as an individual no more to be considered. As he talked, leaning beside me on the window sill, my shoulder brushed against the wooden prop that held up the window sash, and that part of my brain which was concerned with my survival told me to move back into the room and snatch the stick . . . and let the plate-glass weighted sash smash down on his neck . . . and my body obeyed.

"It was horrible, but no more horrible and unreal than the whole nightmare I had begun to inhabit. All I knew was that I must get my letters and that he had prevented me, and now he could prevent me no longer. I went through the drawers of his desk and couldn't find them. I looked everywhere. I even tried to pick the lock of his filing cabinet, with a hairpin from my own head, but it broke off in the lock. I realised the key would be in his pocket, but when I turned back to the window to try and nerve myself to get it, the sense of nightmare lifted, leaving me with the realisation of absolute, hideous fact. I had killed a man and I was afraid. Even then some instinct of self-preservation told me to take with me every trace that I had ever been in the room, and when I had picked up my bag and my gloves I saw the *New Statesman* that had been in my hands as we leaned out of the window pinned under him. I pulled it free and opened the door and ran for my life down the stairs and out into the street with the other ants we had looked at, crawling across the pavement.

"Not to look up as I crossed the street was the hardest thing I ever did; not to look up and see if the horror I had done could be seen from the street. But I didn't look up. I knew all the time that I was saving my life for no purpose; that I should end it myself whether they found me out or not, but first I had to get back my letters and destroy them. And now that is done.

"So while they burn—and I dare not die till they are all burnt—I am writing to you for the last time, because I cannot even now believe that you do not exist; to you, the one creature who would have understood and the only one from whom I should have needed forgiveness. And I shall add it to the pile and watch it crumble to ash before I go myself—while the balance of my mind is disturbed . . ."

But the letter wasn't burnt. She hadn't watched it crumble.

And the room was empty. Marcia wrenched open the door. "I can't find her," she said. "She isn't in the house." She looked deathly frightened. "Does the letter say anything——"

"It isn't really a letter. It's Mabel's attempt to justify herself to her own soul, I think, before she—went away. She meant to destroy it first. She can't have gone yet."

"Unless she was interrupted. If she had seen us coming up the hill——" Marcia stood, for a moment, staring blindly. "If she had seen us coming she wouldn't wait, would she? She would bundle them into the grate and get away before it was too late . . . but where would she go? I've looked in every part of the house—not just called her name, I mean—she mightn't hear. I've searched." Twisting her hands together, she turned back to me. "Simon, where would she go?"

And suddenly I knew where Mabel would go.

I said, "If she'd gone out the back way as soon as she saw us and taken the lane up the hill, we shouldn't have met her, should we?"

"No, but why should she? It doesn't lead anywhere."

"It didn't have to." I took her by the shoulder. "I'd rather go alone."

But Marcia came with me.

She was under the elms when we found her, dead only a little while, huddled face downwards on the kind earth, wearing her green coat. Marcia stood in silence with her face buried in her hands while the elms shuddered and whispered their tale of eternity. My ears, sharpened by the stillness, heard a woodpecker calling somewhere in the far distance and some part of me registered that it sounded too faintly to presage immediate rain.

At last Marcia said, "Simon, what must we do? Have we to tell someone—the police?"

"I suppose so. Nobody will come here. We could go down to the house and telephone."

We began to move slowly. Nearer the house, Marcia said, "You don't have to see me through this, you know. Why don't you go back to town before you get mixed up in it?"

"Because I love you." I spoke without emotion.

"I know." She didn't look at me. Of course she knew. We both knew everything about each other. We seemed to have lived a lifetime and grown old together. There was no restraint between us any more.

"Do you want me to go away?" I asked, but now, at last, I knew the answer, and as we moved down the hill together the woodpecker called again, but this time nearer.

THE PERENNIAL LIBRARY MYSTERY SERIES

E. C. Bentley

TRENT'S LAST CASE
"One of the three best detective stories ever written."
—Agatha Christie

TRENT'S OWN CASE
"I won't waste time saying that the plot is sound and the detection satisfying. Trent has not altered a scrap and reappears with all his old humor and charm."
—Dorothy L. Sayers

Gavin Black

A DRAGON FOR CHRISTMAS
"Potent excitement!"
—*New York Herald Tribune*

THE EYES AROUND ME
"I stayed up until all hours last night reading *The Eyes Around Me*, which is something I do not do very often, but I was so intrigued by the ingeniousness of Mr. Black's plotting and the witty way in which he spins his mystery. I can only say that I enjoyed the book enormously."
—F. van Wyck Mason

YOU WANT TO DIE, JOHNNY?
"Gavin Black doesn't just develop a pressure plot in suspense, he adds uninfected wit, character, charm, and sharp knowledge of the Far East to make rereading as keen as the first race-through."   —*Book Week*

Nicholas Blake

THE BEAST MUST DIE
"It remains one more proof that in the hands of a really first-class writer the detective novel can safely challenge comparison with any other variety of fiction."
—*The Manchester Guardian*

THE CORPSE IN THE SNOWMAN
"If there is a distinction between the novel and the detective story (which we do not admit), then this book deserves a high place in both categories."
—*The New York Times*

THE DREADFUL HOLLOW
"Pace unhurried, characters excellent, reasoning solid."
—*San Francisco Chronicle*

END OF CHAPTER
". . . admirably solid . . . an adroit formal detective puzzle backed up by firm characterization and a knowing picture of London publishing."
—*The New York Times*

HEAD OF A TRAVELER
"Another grade A detective story of the right old jigsaw persuasion."
—*New York Herald Tribune Book Review*

MINUTE FOR MURDER
"An outstanding mystery novel. Mr. Blake's writing is a delight in itself."
—*The New York Times*

THE MORNING AFTER DEATH
"One of Blake's best."
—Rex Warner

A PENKNIFE IN MY HEART
"Style brilliant . . . and suspenseful."
—*San Francisco Chronicle*

THE PRIVATE WOUND
[Blake's] best novel in a dozen years . . . . An intensely penetrating study of sexual passion . . . . A powerful story of murder and its aftermath."
—Anthony Boucher, *The New York Times*

A QUESTION OF PROOF
"The characters in this story are unusually well drawn, and the suspense is well sustained."
—*The New York Times*

THE SAD VARIETY
"It is a stunner. I read it instead of eating, instead of sleeping."
—Dorothy Salisbury Davis

THERE'S TROUBLE BREWING
"Nigel Strangeways is a puzzling mixture of simplicity and penetration, but all the more real for that."
—*The Times Literary Supplement*

THOU SHELL OF DEATH
"It has all the virtues of culture, intelligence and sensibility that the most exacting connoisseur could ask of detective fiction."
—*The Times* [London] *Literary Supplement*

THE WHISPER IN THE GLOOM
"One of the most entertaining suspense-pursuit novels in many seasons."
—*The New York Times*

Edmund Crispin

BURIED FOR PLEASURE

"Absolute and unalloyed delight."

—Anthony Boucher, *The New York Times*

D. M. Devine

MY BROTHER'S KILLER

"A most enjoyable crime story which I enjoyed reading down to the last moment."

—Agatha Christie

Kenneth Fearing

THE BIG CLOCK

"It will be some time before chill-hungry clients meet again so rare a compound of irony, satire, and icy-fingered narrative. *The Big Clock* is . . . a psychothriller you won't put down."

—*Weekly Book Review*

Andrew Garve

THE ASHES OF LODA

"Garve . . . embellishes a fine fast adventure story with a more credible picture of the U.S.S.R. than is offered in most thrillers."

—*The New York Times Book Review*

THE CUCKOO LINE AFFAIR

". . . an agreeable and ingenious piece of work." —*The New Yorker*

A HERO FOR LEANDA

"One can trust Mr. Garve to put a fresh twist to any situation, and the ending is really a lovely surprise." —*The Manchester Guardian*

MURDER THROUGH THE LOOKING GLASS

". . . refreshingly out-of-the-way and enjoyable . . . highly recommended to all comers." —*Saturday Review*

NO TEARS FOR HILDA

"It starts fine and finishes finer. I got behind on breathing watching Max get not only his man but his woman, too." —Rex Stout

THE RIDDLE OF SAMSON

"The story is an excellent one, the people are quite likable, and the writing is superior." —*Springfield Republican*

Michael Gilbert

BLOOD AND JUDGMENT
"Gilbert readers need scarcely be told that the characters all come alive at first sight, and that his surpassing talent for narration enhances any plot. . . . Don't miss." —*San Francisco Chronicle*

THE BODY OF A GIRL
"Does what a good mystery should do: open up into all kinds of ramifications, with untold menace behind the action. At the end, there is a bang-up climax, and it is a pleasure to see how skilfully Gilbert wraps everything up." —*The New York Times Book Review*

THE DANGER WITHIN
"Michael Gilbert has nicely combined some elements of the straight detective story with plenty of action, suspense, and adventure, to produce a superior thriller." —*Saturday Review*

DEATH HAS DEEP ROOTS
"Trial scenes superb; prowl along Loire vivid chase stuff; funny in right places; a fine performance throughout." —*Saturday Review*

FEAR TO TREAD
"Merits serious consideration as a work of art."
  —*The New York Times*

C. W. Grafton

BEYOND A REASONABLE DOUBT
"A very ingenious tale of murder . . . a brilliant and gripping narrative."
  —Jacques Barzun and Wendell Hertig Taylor

Edward Grierson

THE SECOND MAN
"One of the best trial-testimony books to have come along in quite a while." —*The New Yorker*

Cyril Hare

DEATH IS NO SPORTSMAN
"You will be thrilled because it succeeds in placing an ingenious story in a new and refreshing setting. . . . The identity of the murderer is really a surprise." —*Daily Mirror*

Cyril Hare (cont'd)

DEATH WALKS THE WOODS
"Here is a fine formal detective story, with a technically brilliant solution demanding the attention of all connoisseurs of construction."
—Anthony Boucher, *The New York Times Book Review*

AN ENGLISH MURDER
"By a long shot, the best crime story I have read for a long time. Everything is traditional, but originality does not suffer. The setting is perfect. Full marks to Mr. Hare." —*Irish Press*

TRAGEDY AT LAW
"An extremely urbane and well-written detective story."
—*The New York Times*

UNTIMELY DEATH
"The English detective story at its quiet best, meticulously underplayed, rich in perceivings of the droll human animal and ready at the last with a neat surprise which has been there all the while had we but wits to see it." —*New York Herald Tribune Book Review*

WITH A BARE BODKIN
"One of the best detective stories published for a long time."
—*The Spectator*

Robert Harling

THE ENORMOUS SHADOW
"In some ways the best spy story of the modern period. . . . The writing is terse and vivid . . . the ending full of action . . . altogether first-rate."
—Jacques Barzun and Wendell Hertig Taylor, *A Catalogue of Crime*

Matthew Head

THE CABINDA AFFAIR
"An absorbing whodunit and a distinguished novel of atmosphere."
—Anthony Boucher, *The New York Times*

MURDER AT THE FLEA CLUB
"The true delight is in Head's style, its limpid ease combined with humor and an awesome precision of phrase." —*San Francisco Chronicle*

M. V. Heberden

ENGAGED TO MURDER
"Smooth plotting."   *—The New York Times*

James Hilton

WAS IT MURDER?
"The story is well planned and well written."
                                                          —The New York Times

P. M. Hubbard

HIGH TIDE *(available 3/82)*
"A smooth elaboration of mounting horror and danger."
                                                          —Library Journal

Elspeth Huxley

THE AFRICAN POISON MURDERS
"Obscure venom, manical mutilations, deadly bush fire, thrilling climax
compose major opus.... Top-flight."
                                          —Saturday Review of Literature

Francis Iles

BEFORE THE FACT
"Not many 'serious' novelists have produced character studies to com-
pare with Iles's internally terrifying portrait of the murderer in *Before
the Fact,* his masterpiece and a work truly deserving the appellation of
unique and beyond price."   *—Howard Haycraft*

MALICE AFORETHOUGHT
"It is a long time since I have read anything so good as *Malice Aforethought,* with its cynical humour, acute criminology, plausible detail and
rapid movement. It makes you hug yourself with pleasure."
                                          —H. C. Harwood, Saturday Review

Michael Innes

DEATH BY WATER *(available 4/82)*
"The amount of ironic social criticism and deft characterization of scenes
and people would serve another author for six books."
                          —Jacques Barzun and Wendell Hertig Taylor

Michael Innes (cont'd)

THE LONG FAREWELL *(available 4/82)*
"A model of the deft, classic detective story, told in the most wittily diverting prose."
—*The New York Times*

Mary Kelly

THE SPOILT KILL
"Mary Kelly is a new Dorothy Sayers. . . . [An] exciting new novel."
—*Evening News*

Lange Lewis

THE BIRTHDAY MURDER
"Almost perfect in its playlike purity and delightful prose."
—Jacques Barzun and Wendell Hertig Taylor

Arthur Maling

LUCKY DEVIL
"The plot unravels at a fast clip, the writing is breezy and Maling's approach is as fresh as today's stockmarket quotes."
—*Louisville Courier Journal*

RIPOFF
"A swiftly paced story of today's big business is larded with intrigue as a Ralph Nader-type investigates an insurance scandal and is soon on the run from a hired gun and his brother. . . . Engrossing and credible."
—*Booklist*

SCHROEDER'S GAME
"As the title indicates, this Schroeder is up to something, and the unravelling of his game is a diverting and sufficiently blood-soaked entertainment."
—*The New Yorker*

Thomas Sterling

THE EVIL OF THE DAY
"Prose as witty and subtle as it is sharp and clear. . .characters unconventionally conceived and richly bodied forth . . . . In short, a novel to be treasured."
—Anthony Boucher, *The New York Times*

Julian Symons

THE BELTING INHERITANCE
"A superb whodunit in the best tradition of the detective story."
—August Derleth, *Madison Capital Times*

BLAND BEGINNING
"Mr. Symons displays a deft storytelling skill, a quiet and literate wit, a nice feeling for character, and detectival ingenuity of a high order."
—Anthony Boucher, *The New York Times*

BOGUE'S FORTUNE
"There's a touch of the old sardonic humour, and more than a touch of style."
—*The Spectator*

THE BROKEN PENNY
"The most exciting, astonishing and believable spy story to appear in years.
—Anthony Boucher, *The New York Times Book Review*

THE COLOR OF MURDER
"A singularly unostentatious and memorably brilliant detective story."
—*New York Herald Tribune Book Review*

THE 31ST OF FEBRUARY
"Nobody has painted a more gruesome picture of the advertising business since Dorothy Sayers wrote 'Murder Must Advertise', and very few people have written a more entertaining or dramatic mystery story."
—*The New Yorker*

Dorothy Stockbridge Tillet
(John Stephen Strange)

THE MAN WHO KILLED FORTESCUE
"Better than average."
—*Saturday Review of Literature*

Simon Troy

SWIFT TO ITS CLOSE
"A nicely literate British mystery . . . the atmosphere and the plot are exceptionally well wrought, the dialogue excellent."
—*Best Sellers*

Henry Wade

A DYING FALL
"One of those expert British suspense jobs . . . it crackles with undercurrents of blackmail, violent passion and murder. Topnotch in its class."
—*Time*

THE HANGING CAPTAIN
"This is a detective story for connoisseurs, for those who value clear thinking and good writing above mere ingenuity and easy thrills."
—*Times Literary Supplement*

Hillary Waugh

LAST SEEN WEARING . . .
"A brilliant tour de force."
—Julian Symons

THE MISSING MAN
"The quiet detailed police work of Chief Fred C. Fellows, Stockford, Conn., is at its best in *The Missing Man* . . . one of the Chief's toughest cases and one of the best handled."
—Anthony Boucher, *The New York Times Book Review*

Henry Kitchell Webster

WHO IS THE NEXT?
"A double murder, private-plane piloting, a neat impersonation, and a delicate courtship are adroitly combined by a writer who knows how to use the language."
—Jacques Barzun and Wendell Hertig Taylor

Anna Mary Wells

MURDERER'S CHOICE
"Good writing, ample action, and excellent character work."
—*Saturday Review of Literature*

A TALENT FOR MURDER
"The discovery of the villain is a decided shock."
—*Books*

Edward Young

THE FIFTH PASSENGER
"Clever and adroit . . . excellent thriller . . ."
—*Library Journal*